Books by Reneé Porter

Dreamville
Bell Park

The Taliaferro Chronicles
The 13th Victim
Redemption Ridge

Dreamville

A Novel

Reneé Porter

Roet Press   Plantation, Florida

DEDICATION

For Rob, always.

ACKNOWLEDGMENTS

This book was born in the land we all sometimes visit when our real world is "too much with us" as Wordsworth once wrote. It's a world we've all visited whether we want to admit it or not.

Again, I must thank my readers who always inspire me to want to tell one more story, because that's what we writers are – storytellers, who've spun our dreams into tales to capture our audience's attention with the worlds inside our heads, if only for a short time.

I have to thank P.J., my editor, at Roet Press. Thank you for your truth.

This time I have to acknowledge my Rob, not just as the person who gives me his love, but who, this time, gave me the invaluable knowledge of his experience as a psychologist, who helped me to understand just how our brains really work.

And finally, a thank you to those friends who listen, love, and allow me to be obsessed with the people who only come to life in my books.

Reneé Porter

The World Is Too Much With Us

The world is too much with us; late and soon,
Getting and spending, we lay waste our powers;
Little we see in Nature that is ours;
We have given our hearts away, a sordid boon!
This Sea that bares her bosom to the moon,
The winds that will be howling at all hours,
And are up-gathered now like sleeping flowers,
For this, for everything, we are out of tune;
It moves us not. --Great God! I'd rather be
A Pagan suckled in a creed outworn;
So might I, standing on this pleasant lea,
Have glimpses that would make me less forlorn;
Have sight of Proteus rising from the sea;
Or hear old Triton blow his wreathèd horn.

William Wordsworth

Chapter One

I woke up in a strange bed again. Not the first time for me, either. Don't get me wrong. I'm not an easy woman to live with or love. I've always tried to be selective, but I've never wanted ties or romance. I stopped believing in knights in shining armor when I was pushed off my first horse by a knight whose only armor was his arrogance and my naïveté.

Anyway, the room felt odd. It felt comfortable and that was not a feeling I wanted or liked after waking up in some man's bed, especially when I had no idea how I had gotten there. But this room, this room was different because it felt strangely right.

And that was the problem. The bed felt right. It smelled right and the light coming through the window was right. Actually everything was right – except that nothing should be right. After all, I had probably just pulled another stupid stunt by going home with a man I had never met before, unless I had been really stupid and had pulled a encore with someone from my past.

Ok, call me a slut. I know you're thinking it. Whatever. I stopped caring about *that* with that first rough landing from the white knight's horse. I had hardened myself against being hurt ages ago. I felt happy most of the time. I just sometimes fell into bed with a man the way a drunk falls off the wagon. At least I always had the sense to get out of there before morning, before sentiments could be expressed, or even names and numbers exchanged. I saw it as safer that way. No one got hurt. No friends, but benefits when I needed them.

So I dreaded rolling over to see who might be lying behind me. I listened closely for a moment, hoping to god that he wasn't a mouth breather or just another drunk. God, I really had to stop doing this. I was going to get myself in serious trouble, though my gut usually told me who was safe and who was pretending to be safe. Once I had gone home with a man I knew. Big mistake. My gut was overruled by my brain or heart or whatever makes decisions on that one. We weren't at his house more than five minutes before he was drawing lines of coke on his glass table, expecting me to partake, which I did not. Drugs were a sure sign to get out of Dodge. And I did. He sat at his glass table staring with an open mouth as I walked out the door.

I should have known it was a mistake when I saw that glass coffee table. Why do some men think a glass table is a necessary item of decor, by the way? Never could figure that one out. Signs of a bad time to come and a bachelor who would probably throw a woman from a horse – a glass table and man cave furnishings. They were sure signs to leave, even if drugs didn't make an appearance.

Anyway, whomever I had followed home this time was quiet. Warm, but strangely quiet. So I rolled over to discover whatever folly I had committed only to be faced with the sleeping form of a very large Calico cat.

I laughed out loud, startling the cat, who stopped long enough to stretch its body before it bounced from the bed. That was when I had an even more disquieting thought – the cat looked an awful lot like the cat I had had in high school. Chaucer. That was the cat's name. I had been reading *Canterbury Tales* my junior year of high school when I brought the cat home with me. I had liked Chaucer's caustic wit and had named the cat in his honor. I remembered hiding Chaucer in my room for almost a month before my dad discovered him. Of course, my grandmother had been my accomplice in that endeavor.

My father was not happy when he saw the cat, but Chaucer, being a cat, was fickle and chose my father as his person. I smiled thinking about how little time it took Chaucer to win my father over. When I found cat treats in my father's desk drawer, I knew Chaucer would be okay.

The cat I had just seen looked like Chaucer. Too much like Chaucer.

I sat up in the bed and looked around and almost jumped out of the bed the way the cat had. The room was familiar because it was identical to my bedroom I had had in high school. The Sheraton maple dresser on one wall situated next to an old steam radiator painted white. A white brick fire place. Another piece of Sheraton maple furniture in the shape of a desk in the far corner on the other side of the room, complete with schoolbooks and a blue, green and white floral notebook.

I moved down the bed and looked at the wall behind me. I already knew what was there, but I had to check anyway. Yeah, they were there. A collage of *Rolling Stone* magazine covers and photos pasted to the wall.

Motherfucker.

Where was I and how the hell did I get here?

Oh, I guess that I should mention that I often curse like a sailor. Growing up with brothers can do that to you, although I really can't blame them for it. I think I enjoyed the charm of a good old Anglo-Saxon curse. And, while I restrained myself most of the time when conversing with most other people – especially customers, there was always a running dialogue in my head that would make a frat boy blush. People just never expected it from a woman who loved dresses and antiques the way I did.

Cursing aside, I went to the dresser and looked into the mirror and saw my 16 year old face and body. No way. I touched my hair and saw the long, dark brown curls that I had hated when I was sixteen and had learned to love by the time I was thirty.

But there were more than a few problems with waking up in my sixteen year old body, the most notable being that I was thirty two and not sixteen. I sat down on the end of the bed and Chaucer (at least I assumed he was Chaucer), jumped back on the bed next to me. He really looked like Chaucer, down to the brown spot on his forehead between the black and white around his eyes. I absentmindedly rubbed his head between his ears and he purred as he crawled onto my lap.

I was dreaming. That's it. I've always known when I was dreaming so this must be a dream. I pushed the cat off my lap and crawled back under the covers. I decided to sleep again so I could wake back up in my 32 year old body and say to myself, "Wow, that was a weird fucking dream."

But I wasn't going to be allowed that luxury.

The bedroom door opened and my grandmother said, "Get up or you'll be late for school. Your brothers are already waiting and your breakfast will be cold if you dawdle."

My grandmother?

My grandmother.

I was so stunned by her appearance that I automatically jumped out of bed as if a drill sergeant had barked the order at me.

I opened the drawer where I had always kept my clean underwear. There they were. White cotton bikinis. Not a silk thong in sight. Wow. This dream was really a winner in the weirdness category.

I started to looking for a bra for the girls. Few bras and when I looked down, the girls weren't really there, either. I stopped for a moment and looked at the 16 year old body in the mirror. I really didn't need a bra, yet. Well, I didn't when I was 16. No major boobage yet. The girls wouldn't really arrive for another year.

I opened the closet door next to my bed and saw almost a dozen pair of blue jeans next to shirts neatly arranged by colors, although most of them were white. On the closet door was a thick terry robe. I grinned as I remembered that robe. It was made of pink terry cloth and I had worn it until it was in rags. I had loved that robe. But here it was as fresh and soft as if I had just bought it. I buried my face in it and smiled again. Chanel. Well, at least I had had good taste even then. Chanel was still the perfume of choice for my 32 year old body.

One of my brothers yelled from downstairs. Something about being late for practice of some kind.

Ok. Good dream. Incredible details – from the pink robe to the pale yellow walls and cream carpeting and the silver mercury glass candlesticks on the mantle. I stared at them thinking of how much they were worth. I had forgotten I had ever owned those candlesticks and I wondered what had ever happened to them.

So I decided that I'd just go along with the dream. As dreams go, it wasn't that bad so far. I went to the bathroom down the hall, past the yellow wall phone and the scary door to the third floor of the house. That was not a part of the dream that I was happy about. The third floor of that house was what I called a "bad place" as a 32 year old woman. I know it sounds stupid, but in my 32 years I had learned to listen to that inner voice about certain places. And it had saved my life in more than one or two instances.

Instinctively I looked up to see if the latch on the door was closed. It was and I felt better. I didn't want this dream to turn into a nightmare. My 32 year old brain still sometimes dreamed of what was waiting on the other side of the wall of the landing leading to the third floor. I never saw what was there, but I knew it was bad. Very, very bad.

It didn't take me as long as I thought to find my way around the bathroom, find towels in the linen press, my cosmetics on an antique vanity, toothbrush, and deodorant. Everything was exactly where it should be or where it should have been when I was 16. As I pulled out a green and pink tube of Maybelline mascara, I laughed. Some things really didn't change. Outside the bathroom windows I could hear the yells of boys and the sound of a dribbling basketball.

That was right, too. My brothers had all played basketball. If this dream was true to form, it would have them waiting on me to drive them to school where they would practice hoops before homeroom.

Jesus H. Christ, I was really remembering a lot for a dream.

I headed down the stairs and into the kitchen just as my grandmother was placing a plate of scrambled eggs and bacon on the table. God, it smelled good. Had I ever smelled anything in a dream? I couldn't remember that I ever had. I tried to remember an article on lucid dreaming experiments done at Stanford. One of the earmarks that you were dreaming was difficulty in reading. I snatched up the morning newspaper off the table. I had always had trouble reading in dreams. Words always looked like Klingon in my dreams.

Damn.

I could read everything. Maybe it was just the front page. I quickly tore open the paper and looked at the rest of the pages. I could read everything in it. Ok. Maybe this dream was a little different.

Or, maybe it wasn't a dream. Maybe it was something else. Maybe something had happened to my brain. Could I be in a coma? Was my brain bleeding or was I dead? No, I decided. I was dreaming and somehow all these little details had slipped down into my subconscious from whatever part of the brain that controlled memory.

Suddenly the paper was snatched from my hands and my grandmother pointed at the breakfast on the table.

"Miss Pamela April Norris, you do not have time to read. Eat your breakfast and get yourself and your brothers out of here. I don't have time to put up with your lollygagging."

Lollygagging? Had she just said lollygagging? I hadn't heard that word since she had passed away four years ago.

I sat down in the kitchen chair. Hard.

I looked up at her and realized how much I missed her. My mom and dad had both worked and still lived in the same Connecticut town I had grown up in. My dad was a lawyer with a firm in Manhattan, but my mom had a small quilt shop downtown. They were always out the door long before my brothers and I left the house. My grandmother lived with us and had always been there every morning, making sure we had a good breakfast, which made me think of what this breakfast would do to my 32 year old waistline if the food were real. She was there when we came home every afternoon. Sometimes she had made us a cake. Sometimes cookies. But she was always there.

I wanted to cry at how much I had missed her. I had let the memory of so much of how she loved us slip to the back of my brain. But this dream was reminding me. It was telling me to remember.

I decided that this place was "Dreamville", and, since my body wasn't going to bothered by all the calories, I ate everything on the plate as if someone was going to take it away from me. I jumped up from the table, grabbed my books, and hugged my grandmother. She was startled by the hug, but smiled and shooed me away.

"Go now! You're running late. And don't drive too fast!" she called out as I headed out the kitchen door to where my brothers were playing ball.

"About damn time. You've made us miss practice," my brother Rick said. Rick looked oddly at me and seemed a bit disgusted by my presence. I remembered little about our relationship then, probably because of that very reason.

My other two brothers were arguing over points in their game as we loaded ourselves and our books into the old Volvo wagon.

I looked out the driver's window and saw my grandmother in the kitchen window washing up the breakfast dishes. I was beginning to hate this dream. It was reminding me that I never really appreciated just how much she had done for me.

"Damn, April, get the car on the road!" Rick said from the passenger seat.

"I can't wait till I get my license next year and don't have to wait for you all the time."

My brothers Carl and David laughed in the back seat. Carl flipped Rick on the side of the head with his fingers.

"You mean you can't wait to get a car to take out Lucy alone."

"Screw you," Rick said and rubbed his head.

I looked in the rear view mirror and saw my younger twin brothers who were in the eighth grade. Luckily, the middle school was next door to the high school so I didn't have to drive them somewhere else.

This dream was making me crazy. I closed my eyes and thought, "I want to wake up now. I want to wake up now."

I waited and tuned out the voices of my brothers and for a second I couldn't hear anything but the beating of my heart.

"April! Go! You can sleep in class," Rick said.

I opened my eyes and found myself still in the Volvo with my brothers. In my real world, the one outside of this dream, Rick was a stockbroker. Carl had just finished dental school and David was . . . I tried to remember where David was and then the memory felt as if I had been punched in the stomach. I had forgotten him for a moment and then felt the memory in my head like an electric shock. David was dead, too. Just like my grandmother. Well, not like my grandmother, but he was dead. He had driven his truck into a tree when he was 22 and coming home from a party. He hadn't been wearing a seat belt and he had flown through the windshield like someone flying from a cannon. His girlfriend, Sarah, had lived. Barely. She was a paraplegic now.

I looked at David as he laughed at Carl and it hurt so much to see him so young and happy. He was such a joyful boy. Always smiling. Always happy. And dead outside of this dream.

This damn dream. It was nothing but reminders of grief and sorrow.

I slapped the steering wheel and cursed under my breath. David. Grandmother. Both gone. I really wanted to wake up.

Instead, I drove to school as if I had just driven to it yesterday rather than 16 years ago. I pulled into the lot and into my assigned space. My brothers tumbled from the car and started towards the buildings. I sat there and watched them walk away, sure that when I closed my eyes again, that I would wake up in my bed and this painful and sad dream would be over.

I didn't get out of the car for a moment and when I opened my eyes, I saw that Rick had stopped and was staring at me in the car.

For a moment I saw Rick, the impatient stockbroker, his life based on acquiring wealth. Rick, who was starting to lose his hair a little, but was still young. Rick, with a wife and new son. Rick, the brother whom I never really knew..

Just as quickly as I saw him in his future life, he was 15 once more. Tall and gangly, with a cold anger that seethed and burned like frost on your bare hands.

I brushed my hand across my eyes to keep from crying and nodded my head.

"I'll be there. I've just got to make sure I have all my homework."

He ran to the high school and ignored my failure to follow him into the building. I looked in the opposite direction and watched as Carl and David approached the middle school. I seemed to remember that Carl was never the same after David died. It was as if he had lost his ability to smile. David had been his smile, I thought. What would life have been like for Carl if David hadn't died that night? It hurt too much to think about.

Obviously, I wasn't going to wake up anytime soon. But I was 32 and in a 16 year old body. I wasn't even sure what I was supposed to do this morning. The only thing I knew about today was that I had to go in the building and maneuver my way through classes I had long since forgotten. I looked at the school and headed toward the front door as other students rushed past me.

Which way was homeroom? I let my body remember what to do. Through the glass doors, past the trophy case, turn right and go past the school office, past the classrooms and to the staircase on the left where I should ascend the steps, turn right again and find my locker there.

Damn.

What was my locker number? Did it have a combination lock? Okay. Think! The number was 115. Relieved, I walked to it. A combination lock. Shit. I leaned my head on the cold metal and closed my eyes.

Wake up! I screamed inside my head. Wake up!

I opened my eyes. No such luck. Just a long beige metal door with the number 115 at the top and a combination lock on the handle.

Ok. No problem. I'm dreaming. It doesn't matter what numbers I put in. They'll be right or they won't. It's a dream. Did it even matter?

I looked at the black face of the lock and the silver numbers on it. I turned it to 20 and felt a little click, moved it backwards to 30 and felt another click. Good god, I was remembering the real number. I knew what the last one was. I spun the dial back to 5 and pulled down. The lock released and it hung from the handle by the long U shaped arm.

A bell rang over my head and I raised my hands to cover my ears, managing to drop the books in my arms, cursing at the sound. I had forgotten that red klaxon class bell was above my locker.

Motherfucker, I thought, not realizing that I had spoken aloud.

"Wow. Your language gets more colorful by the day," a boy said as he held out the books I had dropped. I could feel myself blushing and flashed an annoyed look. Ok, who the hell was this? He did not sound like the kids I remembered going to school with. Some kind of accent. Did it matter? I was going to wake up any second now anyway. I took the books from him and shoved them in the locker. I noticed a flute case at the bottom of the locker.

"Oh, hell."

I hadn't played a flute since high school.

"Okay, I'm heading on to homeroom. Better get it together before Brown sees you," the boy said and walked away. Who was he? If this dream was so real, where did he come from because I would definitely have remembered his accent if nothing else.

I followed him down the hall, for some reason feeling that he was probably in the same homeroom I was in. Who was my homeroom teacher? Oh, yeah. Brown. Now I remembered whom the boy had been talking about. Brown, the quiet little dictator who handed out geometry homework and bad grades as if they were free candy from Santa at Christmas.

I went in the room and sat down behind the boy. Everyone looked at me strangely.

What? I glared back at their stares. This was a dream so I decided I could be the bitch I would grow up to be.

For a brief second I wondered if this had this turned into one of those dreams where you go to class and realize that you don't have a shirt on, but I looked down and saw that I was fully clothed. I sighed loudly. I was getting so very tired of this dream.

Miss Brown approached me.

"Pamela, is there some reason you're sitting in Howard's seat? Just because he's absent doesn't mean you get to choose where you want to sit."

At that point I was disgusted with this dream, with this new world I had christened "Dreamville". I wanted to wake up. Now! I looked at Brown with as much condescension as my 16 year face could muster. So, I sat in the wrong seat? Who cared? And that was when I decided that since I was dreaming. I did something only the 32 year old woman would do. I responded in kind.

"Oh, hell," I said. "What are you? The fucking chair Nazi? Give us all a break and just call the roll."

I realized then that I was in real trouble. I don't think anyone in the room even breathed. I stepped back, expecting Brown to slap me or at least grab my arm and drag me downstairs to the office. But she did neither, probably because I was almost a foot taller than she was. The image of her trying to drag me down the hall made me giggle out loud and that I knew I was making things worse.

She looked perfectly calm, but her eyes said otherwise. She was royally pissed. She turned her back to me and continued with the roll. I sat back down in the absent Howard's chair and waited. The boy with the funny accent glanced back at me and smiled. I rolled my eyes at him and he faced forward once again. The 32 year old me felt bad about that. He had only been nice. Why was I being such a bitch?

Either way, I knew trouble was coming for my insubordination, even if I were dreaming. Oh well, if it weren't a dream, I had better come up with a reason for my behavior.

And I was right. As I left for my first class, my classmates gave me a wide berth. Only the boy with the accent hung back, arranging his books and papers. My fellow students knew I was in trouble, too. Brown intercepted me at the door and handed me a pink slip instructing me to head to the principal's office.

Oh, hell, when was I going to wake up?

Chapter Two

I was given the pleasure of spending two wonderfully sad, miserable, and sometimes deliriously happy months of being 16 with the mind of a 32 year old woman. It was not easy pretending to be 16 and yet sometimes it was abnormally easy. I spent more time with my parents than I had since I had left for college. I argued the merits of politics and what could happen in the future. I went to my mom's quilt shop after school and helped her, listening to her talk about the fabrics and quilt patterns she loved. I even spent time with my younger brothers except for Rick, whom I assumed was detained by the faceless Lucy. Odd that I didn't remember her face either, though I did remember her presence in Rick's life. As for Carl and David, though they still acted like the adolescent boys they were, I had missed them so much and found myself even trying to play basketball with them which was an epic failure on my part.

I kept expecting to wake up and when I didn't, I decided that wisdom really was the better part of valor and I shut my mouth. Stopped the cursing. Began to behave. No, pretending to be 16 wasn't easy, but being with people I missed was.

And then just as quickly as I had woken up to being 16 in Dreamville, I woke up alone in my apartment and saw my 32 year old body again. For the past two months I had prayed almost every minute that I would wake up. Now that I had, I found that I missed those months more than I ever thought possible.

I called in sick to work that morning. Not a difficult trick since I owned the place. But I really was sick. I felt nauseous and dizzy most of the morning. What the hell had happened to me? When I walked into the kitchen, I saw my cell phone lying on the concrete kitchen counter and grabbed it. Oh joy! Jesus, I never thought I would be so happy to see a cell phone. I turned it on to check the date the way I had grabbed the paper that morning I had woke up in Dreamville to find grandmother's breakfast on the table. It was January 8th. Not a day had passed since I had spent two months in the 16th year of my life.

So it was a dream after all. I sat on a stool at the butcher block island and cursed loudly, almost screaming from the depths of my gut. After calling Brown a fucking chair Nazi in the dream, the cursing had stopped. Well, out loud at least. It still continued inside my head then like a running commentary. It has taken more restraint that I had thought to keep my vocabulary and manners polite.

It had been the most realistic and bittersweet dream I had ever had. I thought of David and my Grandmother and I began to cry. I felt stupid, but I missed them more now than I had since they had died.

On impulse, I hit Rick's name on my phone's contact list and waited for him to answer. Instead, his wife Lisa picked up, saying, "Rick's phone. How are ya this morning, April? Dish on what you did last night after we left you with that delicious Scotsman. I am so in need of living vicariously through your life."

I laughed and then sniffled and wiped the tears away with the sleeve of my yellow silk robe. The Scotsman? Dinner in Little Italy with Rick and Lisa and The Scotsman, Rick's new client. I remembered nothing about him other than the fact that he and Rick had spent most of the evening discussing plans of some sort.

"Nothing. He put me in a taxi outside Benito's. Unfortunately, The Scotsman seemed otherwise preoccupied."

"Hell, that's not a good story. I wanted something juicy. We got no sleep last night. Baby David cried all night with his teeth. I called in sick. I was too tired to go into the city this morning. Anyway, I guess you want your brother. Let me get him."

"Wait, Lisa, I called in sick today, too. Want to go shopping this afternoon? I need some retail therapy."

I heard her pause on the other end of the connection.

"Lisa, are you there?"

"Yeah, I'm just really tired and well, retail therapy's not in our budget right now. You know. I mean . . ."

I had forgotten the conversation with Rick before The Scotsman had shown up. Money problems. Big ones. His firm had taken a bath in the market crash. They were cutting throats there like Johnny Depp in one of his Pirate movies. What an idiot I was. I had been so tied up in the past because of some stupid dream that I had forgotten Rick was in real trouble.

"Listen, Lisa. Is your nanny coming there anyway?"

"Yeah, but April . . ."

"Ok. Here's what we'll do. Meet me at noon at the front of Macy's. We're going to go and forget everything. We'll be the Queens of Denial today. My treat."

Lisa took a deep breath on the other end.

"April, I can't. I don't know how we're going to pay our bills this month. Being the Queen of Denial just makes it worse. I'm sorry, wait, here's Rick. I'll talk to you later."

"Wait, Lisa," I said, but it was too late. Instead of Lisa, I heard my brother's deep voice on the other end. He sounded tired and angry.

"Sorry, Rick. I just wanted to talk to you, but it can wait. Let me know how today goes, ok?"

He sighed. Today was the day of the long knives at his firm. One way or another, the situation there would be resolved.

"Yeah, I'll do that. Was there something else you wanted, April? I don't want to be late today."

"No, no. Just, just call me later. Promise?"

He agreed and I clicked off the phone. I missed the twin brothers with whom I had spent so much of the two months with in Dreamville last night. Rick was the brother who was rarely seen and sometimes cruel. That brother still had all his dreams pinned on getting his license and taking Lucy out alone, the brother who was a bit of a jerk, but never was around much to make my life too miserable.

God, if he lost his job today, he and Lisa were in big trouble. They had put their money in hedge funds and some risky stocks, too. He said his firm had done it and had convinced their associates to do it as well. Told them it was absolutely safe. What morons he worked for. Wouldn't it be wonderful if I could go back and stop him from investing his money that way?

For that matter, wouldn't it be wonderful if I could stop David from getting in that truck? David would be alive. Carl would have a smile again.

I put the phone back on the counter and went back to the bedroom, closed the drapes and crawled back into bed. I couldn't stop thinking about those two months. It would have been wonderful if it had been more than a dream. I might have been able to change things if it hadn't.

Three hours later I woke to the ringing of my house phone. I staggered into the hall and picked it up. Frank, our building's doorman, was on the line saying that a man by the name of Gordon Stewart was here for me.

Gordon Stewart? Who was he? Oh, the Scotsman. What was he doing here? Had I made plans with him the night before? Frankly, I couldn't remember anything from last night except for the two months I had spent in the past.

I told Frank to have him wait five minutes and then send him up. That would give me at least enough time to wash my face and put on some jeans.

By the time The Scotsman rang my doorbell, I had managed to get dressed and start a pot of coffee. I had pulled on a pair of faded Levis, a white cotton tennis sweater, and twisted my dark curls behind my head with a hair tie.

As I went to answer the door, I wondered if I should have made tea, instead.

Fuck it, I thought. I needed coffee. He could go find tea somewhere else.

When I opened the door, I saw one of the rarest things I had seen in years – a man at least five inches taller than me. Being almost 6 feet tall had both its advantages and disadvantages. I could reach almost any shelf by just stretching my arm upwards. I could also scare away many a man the minute I put on a pair of Jimmy Choo's. Meeting a man that much taller than me was not only unusual, it was almost a miracle.

And he was a man with a smile that seemed to light up the room. How had I not remembered this man from last night? Tall (thank you, lord), beautiful smile, wavy brown hair and laughing grey eyes.

"Gordon. Sorry, migraine this morning. I'm usually not so scattered. Come in."

"You look great. Sure you weren't taking a mental health day?" he said as he followed me into my kitchen and sat down at the island.

"Would you like something with your coffee, like a hit in the head with the migraine hammer?" I said drily.

"Ok. Sorry. You just look well rested. I'll refrain from any more questions concerning you and your migraine," he said, holding his hands up defensively.

I smiled and put a mug of coffee down in front of him.

"I don't remember making plans last night. In fact, how did you know I was even home?"

He sipped the bitter coffee and frowned.

"You wouldn't happen to have any cream or sugar about, would you?"

"Sorry. Didn't think." Yes I did, I thought, but I was being a bitch.

Why? I took a restaurant sugar pourer from the counter and grabbed an open carton of half and half from the fridge.

"No, we didn't have plans," he said. "Your brother told me you were staying home today. He's the one who gave me your address this morning and told me he thought you were, uh, "playing hooky"?

He poured at least two tablespoons of sugar and almost as much creamer into the coffee as he spoke.

"Like a little coffee with your sugar?" I asked.

Again. Where was this bitchiness coming from? My whole world was off-kilter right now. He was being perfectly nice and I was being perfectly rude.

"I apologize. I'm being very rude. Bad night. Really bad night," I said.

He waved his hand above the counter and shook his head.

"It's alright. I did surprise you with my visit. And I was rude last night when I monopolized your brother with business concerns."

"Maybe we can start over. Hello, Ms. Norris. My name is Gordon Stewart. I am very pleased to make your acquaintance."

I laughed and walked to the sink to rinse out my coffee mug and set it in the sink. I leaned against the counter and folded my arms across my chest as I realized that Mr. Stewart was taking a little inventory on his own.

"So what does bring you here, then, Mr. Stewart?"

He shook his head as he swallowed a drink of the sugar coffee he had created.

"Gordon. Please."

"Pamela," I said.

He looked confused for a moment. "I thought your name was April?"

I returned to the stool and sat down.

"To my family and close friends, it is April. April is my middle name. Pamela is my first name," I said. There. A boundary established with this stranger.

"Pamela," he said. "I shan't make that mistake again."

Damn. I was being a bitch again. What was it about this guy?

"It's ok. Call me April. Everyone does, actually."

"No, no. I stand corrected.. As to my visit, after spending the morning with your brother, I thought I might visit your shop, but he informed me you would be out today. I'm buying a flat here and I was going to ask you to help me furnish it."

I inwardly cursed. Now I had not only insulted him, but possibly cost Rick a client and myself a customer.

"Look, I'm sorry. I really am not like this. My brother was kind enough to recommend me and I act like a complete . . ."

I stopped myself before my normal colorful language sprang out of my mouth.

"Bitch?" he completed for me.

At that, I laughed hard. He was definitely not deserving of my attitude. In fact, I liked his attitude.

"Ok, I deserved that. I assume your business with my brother went well this morning since you're looking for a place in Manhattan."

He nodded. "Oh yes, I hired him away from his firm this morning and I believe he's setting up new offices for me this afternoon."

I stood up and almost knocked over the carton of cream.

"What? Did you just say you "hired" him away from his firm? Why? What exactly do you do?"

I felt very protective of my brother right now as if he was being a jerk. And if this man was playing some kind of game with him . . .

"No need to worry. I have some land holdings and a small firm that I'd like to establish a New York office. Your brother's firm is collapsing. I believe you're aware of that. I felt I could trust him so I hired him to run my business affairs here in the states."

I raised one eyebrow at this.

"And I do have enough money to pay him what he was making at his former employer's. So, as this afternoon isn't what either of us planned since I just turned up at your door out of the blue, could we make plans for tomorrow?"

It was my turn to nod. I felt very chastised. I had been a complete bitch to him and he not only wanted to hire me, he was already Rick's new employer. And salvation, if I were truthful.

As he stood to leave and I followed him to my apartment door, I reached out my hand to shake his. He looked down at my open hand with a little bit of a crooked smile.

I liked him, but I refused to let him know more than that open hand of friendship.

"Tomorrow will be fine. What time?"

"How about 9:30 tomorrow morning at your shop?"

I smiled in agreement. He took my hand and shook it.

I waited until I heard the elevator door close before I gave out a little whoop of celebration and ran to the phone to call Rick and April.

Chapter Three

What I hadn't planned on was dreaming again.

I had talked to Rick and then April for over an hour, getting all the details on Mr. Gordon Stewart. It seems that he had rescued Rick. Rick's firm was not just firing brokers. They were filing for bankruptcy and closing their doors. Of course, Rick had known nothing of this and was tearing his head up wondering what the 10 a.m. conference would reveal about the company's future when Mr. Stewart had shown up for his 9 a.m. appointment.

But Stewart had known and had made his proposal immediately. Rick was stunned that the company was filing for bankruptcy, but gladly welcoming of the new home and opportunity. True, he and Lisa had lost their savings, but thanks to Stewart, Rick would have a chance to start over and his family would not suffer too much.

I went to bed that night so happy that I had forgotten about my "two month" dream excursion into my past.

Another big mistake on my part.

The minute my head hit the pillow, I was in the past again. Unfortunately, I was on the staircase to the third floor with the door closed behind me. I could sense someone or something standing on the steps on the other side of the landing and I could hearing raspy breathing and the slow footsteps of someone dragging something heavy behind them.

I almost fell down the oak staircase trying to get to the closed door, terrified that it was latched on the outside, but the door opened and I flew into the hall, slammed the door shut and latched it as quickly as I could.

Shit. I was dreaming again. And this time Dreamville was coming very close to becoming a nightmare.

I almost jumped five feet when I felt someone tap me on my shoulder. I whirled around to see David standing behind me at the door to his and Carl's bedroom.

"April, what were you doing upstairs?" he asked.

He was as afraid of that part of the house as I was, but he would never admit it to our brothers. Their derision would have been unending.

"David, you scared me to death."

I looked at him and realized he wasn't 14 anymore. This David was at least 16 and taller than I was. Oh hell, I was definitely dreaming again. I looked upward and thought, 'What, last night wasn't enough?'

"April?"

"Sorry, David. I thought I saw a mouse on the landing."

He went to the open stairwell to the first floor and started down the steps.

"Better tell Dad so he can get an exterminator here. I've gotta head to work. See you at supper," he said and was gone.

I shivered although I could see through the bank of windows on the second floor landing that it was full summer outside. The foliage was thick and deep green in the woods around our house.

Dreaming again. What was going on?

Was anything in my life real? Was I 32 or what, 19 or 20 now? If David was 16 or 17, then I was at least 19. I needed to find a newspaper and find out the date. I took another look at the locked door and could sense that thing on the other side of it. I put my hand on the door. Nothing. Just white enamel paint on old oak. I took a deep breath and was removing my hand when I looked down and saw the doorknob turning very slowly. I ran downstairs as fast I had left the third floor staircase and found myself alone in the house. The morning paper was always on the kitchen table and I headed there to see the date. I hoped it wasn't in Klingon. I really needed to know what was going on.

Yeah, dreaming again. It was three years later than the last dream and if I were correct in my calculations, I was home from college for the summer. I glanced at the clock and saw that it was after 9 a.m.

Where was everyone? I knew my mom and dad were at work, but where were Carl and Rick and my grandmother? And what was I supposed to be doing that day? Had I had a summer job then? What had I done that summer, much less that day?

One thing I knew I would not have been doing was going up the steps to the third floor. The only time I had gone up there was to help my mom carry boxes upstairs for storage. There were three spare bedrooms up there, but I couldn't remember anyone ever using them except for a distant relative visiting around the holidays.

Ok, if this dream follows the last one, then I had better figure things out fast. I needed to remember everything I could about that summer. If I were stuck in this dream again, I didn't want to walk around acting like an idiot.

I saw the calendar on the kitchen wall next to the red touchtone wall phone above a Formica bar. I walked over to it to look for clues about this day. I needed to be able to read if this dream were like the last one. I saw my grandmother had penciled in a doctor's appointment for that morning. Well, that explained her absence and David had said something about going to work. Where had he worked the summer before his junior year? The country club pool as a lifeguard. That explained his leaving for work so late.

Just as I was taking a mental inventory of my 19th summer, my brother Rick came through the door and slammed a set of keys on the counter,

"Get out of my way so I can call Mom," he said and pushed me backwards.

I started to cuss at him and stopped myself. I had a slight memory that this summer would be bad for him more than I did for myself. He had just graduated and was leaving for college in the fall. He had gotten a basketball scholarship at Maryland. Lucy had dumped him right after graduation and his summer had been lonely and fairly miserable. If she hadn't dumped him yet, she would in the next week or so. Bitch, I thought, but then I smiled, remembering Lisa and baby David. But, I still didn't like that Rick was about to be hurt. Even if he were a jerk most of the time, I didn't like this Lucy anymore now than I had when I had been 16.

"You know, she's not the one," I said without thinking.

"What are you talking about?" he said and slammed the receiver back on the wall cradle. "Mom's line is busy and that stupid old car we got when you left won't start. Now Lucy has another reason to get mad at me."

He was halfway across the kitchen before he realized what I had said. He turned to me with an angry and scared looked on his face.

"What did you just say?"

I hesitated and wondered if I told him the truth if it would change anything. Oh hell, this was a dream so none of it mattered.

"I said that she's not the one."

He rushed toward me and his anger was overwhelming his common sense. I briefly thought that he would strike me for having dismissed Lucy as someone for whom he should not care.

"How the hell do you know? You don't even have a boyfriend since Vince dumped you before spring break. Lucy loves me. You don't know shit."

Vince? Oh god, yes, Vince. I was starting to remember a Vince. He was the one I thought I was in love with, the one I thought was the knight on the white charger, the one who had dumped me before he and his friends took off for Florida for spring break. I think he had hurt me. At least my broken memory told me he had. I guess I had to admit that. It had must have been bad. Yes, I thought. It was bad. It had been bad enough to keep me running from commitment for most of my twenties. Vince, who was always there when he needed a date and conveniently absent the rest of the time. Vince, who left me sitting by the phone *a lot*, who forgot our dates and then showed up with a single rose to show me how much 'he cared' and then apologized for not calling. And I always took him back. What an idiot I had been.

It was only after he dumped me that one day I passed a man selling roses at an intersection near my dorm. I realized I had spent the last months crying over a cruel bastard who saw me only as a convenience.

Rick's words reminded me of the sting of the humiliation I had felt, especially after bringing Vince home to meet my family at Thanksgiving. I had never been in love, not even in high school, so having my heart stomped on would have been devastating if Vince hadn't flunked out of college that semester and hadn't returned after spring break. It was as if he had just vanished. Not seeing him on a daily basis had made it easier, but the summer I was 19, I guess I had still been hurting.

Of course, the 32 year old me had forgotten most everything about Vince except for the fact that I had learned not to trust most men after that. The 32 year old me didn't care the way the 19 year old me had. Some men made me feel like a snapping turtle. If they got too close, I snapped and withdrew into that hard shell I had built around myself.

So what did I say to Rick, who was about to be dumped by Lucy? Did I tell him that he would meet Lisa in his junior year of college and that he would fall head over heels for her, that they would buy a house on Long Island and have a beautiful boy whom they named David after our dead brother?

Hell, no, I couldn't say all that. Dream or no dream. I didn't know when I was going to wake up. That made me think about the migraine I had woke up with that morning. Maybe something was really wrong and I needed to see a doctor when I woke up. Mental note to dreaming April – see a doctor when you wake up!

"Sorry. Sorry. Of course, Lucy loves you," I said and walked outside to the pool and noticed Mom and Dad's Jacuzzi.

Now that was one more detail than I wanted to remember. I had a vague vision of having sex with Vince in that Jacuzzi late Thanksgiving night after everyone else had gone to bed. Eww.

Thinking about that made me want to drain the damn thing and take a scrub brush and a bottle of cleanser to it. I laughed, remembering how awkward that sex with him had been. Vince was a horrible lover, but it would be several years and several lovers after he dumped me that I came to know that. Vince was definitely a glass table, man cave type of guy. I wondered what he was doing now in my non-

Dreamville. Probably married with a passel of kids somewhere.

I looked up at the blue sky and said a silent "Thank you" for being dumped by him. Now that would have been the worst "big" mistake I would have ever made if I had married him.

I was sitting on the side of the pool with my legs dangling in the heated water. I wondered if I had a swimsuit in my room. I had missed swimming outside. The club I belonged to in Manhattan had an Olympic size pool, but it wasn't the same as floating in this small pool with the sun on my face, the green woods and blue sky surrounding me.

Rick came out the back door and pulled a redwood chair over to where I sat. He squinted at the woods beyond the pool.

I looked down at my feet in the water and the ripples that spread out from them as I slowly moved my feet in circles. An apple blossom moved out and away on the top of the water.

"You can use my car if you want," I said to Rick, though I had no idea where my keys might be, much less where I had parked the car. I did remember that my folks had bought me a little Honda when I graduated, though I never used it. I had left for Columbia the year before and keeping a car in Manhattan was absurdly expensive.

I knew that they had really bought it for Rick because he used it when I wasn't home, but now that I was home for the summer, he was stuck with the old Volvo.

He picked up a stone from the deck and tossed it across the pool into the woods.

"Doesn't matter. She went to the lake with her 'friends.' I think you were probably right about her," he said and sighed.

I pulled my legs from the water and turned to face him. What to say to him? The truth was out, but since I was in Dreamville, did it really matter?

"Then dump her. You're going to meet so many great people in the next few years. You'll have forgotten her in no time at all."

He sneered at me. "You mean the way you've forgotten Vince?"

Now it was my turn to sigh.

"Yes, the way I'm forgetting Vince. Dump her and go enjoy the summer. You know it's going to happen anyway. She's always ordering you around. Why do you let her?"

"I don't know," he mumbled.

"If you're forgetting Vince, how come you were crying the other night?"

"I don't know," I said. "I get moody. I'm a girl. Girls cry. What can I say?"

"Yeah, I've heard you cry maybe three times in my life. Bullshit. You were crying over that asshole."

I stood up and put my hands on my hips and looked out at the woods where he had been staring.

"Does it matter what I think? You asked. Don't turn things around just because it's convenient for you to deflect your own feelings at me."

He stared at me open mouthed.

"What the hell are you talking about? You sound like you've spent too much time with those people at Columbia the way you're talking."

Oops. Mistake. 32 year old me talking instead of 19 year old me. I really had to watch my vocabulary. I sighed again. Boy, did I want to wake up now.

Rick was still staring at the woods.

"What are you looking at over there?"

He stood up next to me and was at least four inches taller. Still skinny, but basketball in Maryland would change that as well as his gym membership.

"That guy who was in your homeroom. His family's going back overseas since he went back to go to school there. I think he's back for the summer. I was just watching the movers."

I shaded my eyes, but couldn't see through the dense greenery. I had no idea whom he was talking about. Maybe it was that kid in my dream last night, the one who hadn't belonged, well at least the one I didn't remember from school. I didn't remember anyone living on the other side of the woods, much less a house over there, but then I had been obsessed with escaping to Columbia the year before. If someone had built the Taj Mahal there, I probably wouldn't have paid much attention.

I shrugged my shoulders and headed back toward the house to change for a swim.

"Listen, take my keys and go out to the lake. I'm not planning on going anywhere today and I'll call Dad about the Volvo so he can get it fixed. Ok?"

He plunged his hands in his jeans pockets and said, "Yeah, thanks," but watched the apple blossom floating across the surface of the pool. I knew he wasn't going to dump her. What was I thinking? It's a dream. I can't change the past in a dream.

I went back upstairs to my bedroom and glanced at the locked third floor door before scuttling into my own bedroom and away from that door. Chaucer was lying on my old desk, sunning himself. He looked up at me and then began to lick his paws and rub his face with them.

Why hadn't I gotten a cat after Chaucer? Probably for the same reason I hadn't had a steady boyfriend since Vince. Easier with no commitments, even to cats, birds and most life forms. I remembered one date several years ago in the land of waking who had said that I cared more about American antiques than I did people. He was partially right. I certainly cared more about them than I did him. He had been the closest I had come to anything resembling a relationship and he had bored me to tears. He had been involved in hedge funds or some kind of stock business and had monotonously talked about them almost all the time except when we were having sex. The last night I had spent with him I had watched his face in the dimness of his bedroom as we were having sex. His eyes were tightly closed, but I kept thinking that he was concentrating on the day's stock numbers the way Woody Allen had said in *Annie Hall* that he thought about baseball stats. That was enough for me. I wanted to be with a man who thought about me, rather than how to prolong his orgasm. I dumped him that night and it had not been pleasant.

But he was wrong about the people part. I cared fiercely about my family. Did it make me a bad person that my interpersonal relationships with non-familial people were practically non existent? I didn't think so then and I didn't now. If I found someone, fine. If not, fine. The last thing I wanted was to go through a messy divorce the way so many of my friends had.

I rummaged through the dresser drawers and found a neon pink bikini. The neon pink was not something that I would be caught dead in as a 32 year old, but at 19, it was perfect for an afternoon alone in the backyard pool and I was surprised that the color wasn't that horrible on my skin. As I was changing, Chaucer sat up and growled at the ceiling. As I finished clasping the neck strap, I walked over to where he sat and looked up and listened. There was a scratching sound coming from the ceiling as if something were trying to get through the plaster ceiling.

Suddenly Chaucer let out the most blood curdling scream and ran to hide under the bed. The cat's scream scared me as much as waking up on the third floor stairs had.

I got down on my hands and knees and lifted the bed skirt.

"Here, kitty. It's ok. Come on," I said and held my hand out to him, wiggling my fingers. Instead of coming to me the cat's ears flattened and he hissed and ran further under the bed, getting as far away from me as possible.

Puzzled, I stood up and wondered what had spooked him. Unfortunately, that was also when I looked in the mirror and saw the woman standing next to me.

Chapter Four

I jumped over the bed and screamed, tripping over my own feet and landing hard on the carpet. I looked up to the door and then to the mirror to see if the woman was still there.

Gone, just as fast as she had appeared. I closed my eyes and started chanting, "I want to wake up," over and over. But, just as in the past dream, nothing happened. I was still firmly 19.

I crawled over to the door, quickly stood and ran down the stairs and outside to the pool as fast I could. I jumped into the water and watched the house, waiting to see if the woman I had seen had followed me. I thought about looking up to the third floor windows, but decided against it. No use tempting fate.

What the hell was that about? I definitely knew nothing like that had ever happened to me when I had been 19 or any other age, for that matter. This was more than just a dream. It was a nightmare first class.

Why was everything exactly as it was when I was 19 except for the third floor and the woman? There were other little things that didn't fit, but I couldn't grasp what they were, except for the house across the way being emptied where no house had stood before, where a boy lived that I couldn't remember except for the dream I had had last night. Why couldn't I remember these things? Or maybe my mind was making it all up to try to tell me something. One thing was sure - I was not going back into that house until another member of my family came home.

Then I thought of Rick. I had screamed like a banshee. He couldn't have left yet so why hadn't he heard me?

I climbed out of the pool and walked over to the driveway where both my Honda and the old Volvo still sat. Where the hell was Rick?

Turning the corner of the house I found him bouncing a basketball around the side of the house.

"Rick!" I yelled.

"What now?" he said.

"Didn't you hear me?"

"Hear you what?" he said and jumped to sink a basket.

I realized that whatever had happened in my bedroom might only have happened in my dream. Somehow the past and what I was seeing weren't converging. Whatever it was, he had been oblivious to it. And there was no way he could not have heard my scream. Just as I was about to head back around the house, the kid with the accent walked up the drive to Rick. At least I think he was the kid. He didn't look like a skinny 16 year old anymore, but he was staring at me like one.

Oh damn. I was standing in the driveway in a neon pink bikini meant to show off the girls that had finally arrived my senior year of high school. Before he could say a word, I ran back around the house and dove into the pool. When I surfaced, I could barely hear my brother and him talking. He must be the guy my brother had been talking about whose family was moving.

Well, good. One more anomaly for this dream. I floated on my back and looked up at the pale sky overhead. I hoped my grandmother would be home soon. I didn't want to spend anymore time here than I had to. And how was I going to sleep tonight? The thought of going back in that bedroom terrified me.

Oh shit, this was a dream. It was Dreamville. None of this was real. Nothing. But what if it wasn't? What if there was a rational explanation for everything, such as me being in a coma or something? Time travel? That made me laugh out loud. If I were traveling in time, then I certainly wouldn't have picked being 16 or 19 as times to where I'd want to travel. But what if I weren't controlling anything? What if I weren't in control of the dream, or time traveling, or whatever was happening.

The voice of Rod Serling's Twilight Zone narration bounced around in my head. Another dimension? Another version of what my life could be like? And what if the thing on the third floor or the woman in the bedroom were trying to tell me something?

And why had Chaucer reacted so strangely? Had he seen the woman before I had? None of it made sense. No. I was dreaming and just like the last time, I would wake up. I tried to remember if I had done anything in the last dream that might have changed my life now, other than call Brown a 'chair Nazi', but couldn't think of anything.

No, it had to be a dream. That would explain all the craziness, including the third floor, the woman, and the guy living in a house where no house had ever been according to my memory.

And my memory was excellent. I had majored in history and then had done my masters in museum studies, though I didn't really want to work in a museum. By that time, I had decided to open one of the best American antique shops in Manhattan. I used a small loan from my folks, found a place in Soho, and had scoured the states south of New York for items, knowing that New England had been picked over for the past 30 years. But in some of the southern states, there were still treasures left that I could afford to buy and resell to New Yorkers. It was an eclectic shop, but it was strictly American. That was my only rule. I called the place Americana Applied and had struggled for a few years to make ends meet.

Unbeknownst to my landlord or my family, I spent those first few years sleeping on a small cot in the back of the cavernous shop, not being able to afford a place of my own yet. But I was determined to succeed and by the time my Dreamville traveling had begun, I had three employees, and had purchased a condo in Soho not far from my shop.

Everything had been going well for me until last night. Now I was seriously worried that I might be ill, or even worse, if not ill, then losing my grip on reality.

I tired of the pool and climbed out to stretch out on one of the cushioned redwood chaise lounges. I shivered a moment, but decided against going back into the house or back to where Rick was still talking to the strange guy and I let the sun slowly warm my skin. Without realizing how tired I was, I drifted off to sleep.

Chapter Five

I woke once more in my own bed, shivering worse than I could ever remember. My teeth were chattering and my hair was wet and cold, my skin hot and hurting.

Shit. I was sick. What time was it?

I looked at the clock on my nightstand and it said 10 a.m.

Ah, hell, I had been scheduled to meet the Scotsman, what was his name? Oh, right, Gordon Stewart, at 9 a.m. I tried to stand and the room began to swirl a bit and I could feel my stomach about to release any contents it held.

I barely made it to the bathroom in time. My skin felt so hot. I was running a fever. I must have gotten a bug of some kind. I struggled to my feet and stood at the sink to wash my face and brush my teeth and mouth out. As I reached to open the mirrored antique cabinet, I was stunned to see that I was sunburned. Badly.

I touched the reflection with one hand and my cheek with the other. My face hurt and I looked down to see that my arms and hands were just as burned.

What the hell? How did I get a sunburn? The last thing I remembered was going to bed.

Oh, yes, and then I remembered my little jaunt to Dreamville and lying on the chaise next to the pool. No way. No damn way did I get sunburned in a dream.

I became dizzy again and barely managed to rinse my mouth out before passing out on the bathroom tile. The last thing I remembered was looking at the New York subway tile I had chosen to use in my bathroom and wondering why there was red blood dripping from edge of the pedestal sink.

I don't know how long I lay there. I remembered hearing voices and being carried back to my bed. I remembered sirens and after awhile I woke to find myself in a hospital ER bed surrounded by curtains with an IV in my arm.

I groaned and felt my whole body ache.

"Don't move too much. You've got a really bad burn and you're dehydrated," a nurse in green scrubs said.

I now saw that my body was covered with some kind of shiny ointment. The burn didn't explain the pain under my right eye. I reached up and touched it to find stitches just below my cheekbone.

I tried to sit up, but realized that I was undressed except for a bandage around my breasts and a pair of neon pink swim bottoms.

"I'm thirsty. Can I have some water?"

"You can have some ice chips," she said and clicked her pen as she attached the plastic clip board to the end of the bed.

"You really shouldn't use those tanning beds. This is what happens if you stay in one too long."

I shook my head as I took an ice chip into my mouth.

"I don't use tanning beds," I said.

She raised her eyebrows and looked down at the burn on my body.

"Well that didn't happen in New York in January."

"How did I get here? Did I have a phone? I need to call my brother."

She adjusted the IV drip and looked at me sternly.

"You really don't remember?"

I shook my head and felt the coolness of the ice against my lips. I touched them with my hand and they were cracked and dry.

"The last thing I remember was waking up and feeling sick. I think I may have passed out in the bathroom, but I know I did not go near a tanning bed last night. What happened to me?"

She headed to the closed curtain.

"The doctor will be in a few minutes. Your family is here as well as the man who brought you in. I can send in your sister, but I'd say you'd prefer the men don't come in yet."

I nodded, not bothering to tell her that I didn't have a sister. I assumed she meant Lisa. I closed my eyes again, determined not to go back to sleep.

Why was I sunburned and why was I still wearing the neon pink bikini bottoms? I must have fallen asleep next to pool in my dream, but that didn't explain why in my real world, I had awoken sunburned in a pink swimsuit, with wet hair and feeling very ill.

Lisa slipped through the curtain and stood next to me.

"Are you feeling better?" she asked.

I nodded and tried to sit up, but found the cloth sheets painfully scratchy against my skin.

"Here, let me raise the head of the bed," she said and pushed the buttons on the bed control.

"How did I get here, Lisa? I don't remember anything but waking up feeling sick."

"Mr. Stewart. When you didn't show up for your appointment, he went over to your building. When your doorman tried to call you, he and Stewart went up to your apartment and found you lying in the bathroom floor, passed out and your face bleeding."

I touched my cheek again and winced.

"I must have hit it when I fell."

"And you don't remember anything," she asked.

"No. I remember talking to you about Rick going to work for, god, why do I keep forgetting his name?"

"Going to work for Stewart. Right? Anyway, after I talked to you, I went to bed. I had a nightmare and I must have overslept. I woke up around 10 a.m. and felt sick. That's it."

She sat down in a chair next to the bed and looked down before looking at me. I knew what was coming next. They had made it quite clear how they felt about my dates.

"Are you sure you didn't go out last night after we talked, maybe meet someone and go home with him? I'm not judging. Don't get mad, but you sometimes do that."

I sighed. No one would believe me if I told them where I had been. Hell, I didn't believe it, except that the bad sunburn and the neon bikini bottoms were telling me a different story entirely.

"No. And do you seriously think I would put on a pink neon bikini? I went to bed and woke up sick. Why doesn't anyone believe me?"

She started to reach out to take my hand and then stopped herself.

"Sorry. It's just none of it makes sense. They said only a tanning bed would do this. Maybe someone gave you a roofie and put you in a tanning bed."

"And then took me home and put me in my bed? Come on, Lisa. That doesn't make any sense either. The security tapes. If that's what happened, then it would show up on the tapes."

I struggled to sit up. I was in pain, but I was feeling stronger. I wanted out of here and I wanted to go home.

"Where are my clothes? I want to leave."

Lisa blushed and pointed at the bikini.

"This is all I had on? Seriously?"

She nodded. "That and the bra top that matched it, but the ambulance crew cut the top off. You had bled all over it."

"There's a police woman outside who wants to talk to you. I think they want to do a rape kit. They're treating this as a potential sex crime since you have no memory of the last 12 hours.

"Shit, a rape kit? Does anyone really think that someone did this to me?"

Lisa took my hand this time and tried to soothe me.

"They were waiting for you to wake up. No one knew anything and they hoped you could tell them something. I'm supposed to bring the policewoman in. Are you sure you're ready for this? I'll stay with you if you want."

I said yes. I knew they would find nothing, but worst of all I now knew that my trips to Dreamville weren't really dreams. You don't wake from a dream wearing the bikini you were wearing when you fell asleep in the sun in the dream. Somehow, someway, I had traveled back to my 19th year. The thought of that sounded absurd, even in my head. Time traveling in my sleep? If I didn't hurt so much, I would have laughed out loud. No doubt. I was losing it.

Yet, somewhere deep within my heart, I knew it was true as sure as I knew that I hadn't been raped by some idiot with a tanning bed.

After the policewoman finished, I asked Lisa for a hospital gown. I needed to talk to Rick. Last night in my visit to Dreamville, I might have changed his past. It was my only proof that I wasn't losing my mind. I knew I didn't dare tell anyone what was really going on, but one simple question might help me.

Rick entered the room with Lisa and I asked her if I could talk to him alone.

"Jesus, April, whoever did this to you, we'll find them. I'm so sorry."

"It's ok, Rick. I'm ok. You know me. I'm strong. Remember, I never cry?"

He took my hand and squeezed it. I winced, but squeezed his back.

"Rick, I'm going to ask you what will seem like a truly stupid question, but I need to know what you remember."

"Ok. Anything."

I took a deep breath. Here goes nothing, I thought.

"Do you remember the summer after you graduated from high school, when you were dating Lucy?"

He paused for a minute and I could see the thoughts turning over in his memory.

"Yeah, the Volvo crapped out on me and I spent most of the summer with you or Stew."

"Stew?"

"Yeah, remember the first day you were home, you told me to dump Lucy? I did that day. Remember, she went out to the lake and I spent the afternoon playing ball with Stew. You spent most of the afternoon in the pool."

He laughed. "I remember Stew kept wanting to go for a swim, too, but I think he wanted to see you. Anyway, Lucy didn't even seem to care. You had been right about her. Stew had come back to close up his family's place and we hung out most of the summer, the three of us. Don't you remember?"

"Rick, who the hell is Stew?" I asked.

"Stew. The guy who found you. We all went to high school together. Gordon Stewart. He was in your homeroom, remember?"

I sat straight up in bed, shocked to the core of my being.

"You mean the skinny kid with the accent was Gordon Stewart?"

"God, April, you must have really hit your head. Yes. Stew. We all called him Stew then. I still do. He's the one who found you."

Chapter Six

How could I forget Gordon Stewart?

I was more confused than ever. No way was Gordon Stewart, the Scotsman, the man who had sat in my kitchen yesterday, the same skinny kid I had seen in Dreamville. But what stunned me even more than that was that Rick had dumped Lucy instead of her dumping him. I had somehow made a small change in the past. Was Gordon Stewart the ripple effect?

Ok. I thought. Then who was the woman in my room? Who or what was on the third floor? If Gordon Stewart were the ripple effect of something as innocuous as telling Rick to dump Lucy, then what were the effects of the other anomalies?

It scared me. Had I changed anything else?

Before I could ask Rick anything else, Gordon Stewart stuck his head through the curtain and asked if he could come in.

Rick stood up and waved him in.

"Come on, Stew. I think she's starting to feel a little better. I'm going to go check on Lisa. Listen, Stew, thanks again. I owe you," he said and patted Stewart on the shoulder as he left.

"I'll be back in a little while, sis. We're waiting for the doctor to decide whether to release you or keep you."

Gordon Stewart walked over to the chair Rick had vacated and sat down.

"You know there are easier ways of not spending time with me," he said and smiled.

I still could not match his face with the face of the kid I had last seen in Dreamville. He was extraordinarily handsome, with the most beautiful grey eyes. Those eyes. I remembered them from my kitchen yesterday in real time. How could I have forgotten them from knowing him when he was 19? This was not a man easily forgotten. Once you saw him, you remembered him forever. His dark curly hair, his broad, muscular shoulders and his incredible heather blue-grey eyes, that seemed to change shades with his mood.

No, I would have remembered him. I remembered everything. I think I would have remembered him, even as a skinny young man.

"Yes, I got first degree burns, stitches in my face and a total loss of memory just to avoid you."

Shit. I was being a bitch to him again. What was it about him that made me so angry? Every time he said something to me, I had to come up with some sharp retort.

"Well, let me know the next time and you can avoid all this," he said and laughed, though his eyes weren't very amused.

"I'm sorry. I don't know what happened, but I thank you for finding me. I don't mean to be so cross. I haven't been myself lately."

He shook his head and then stood up.

"No problem. And don't apologize. You've been through a lot. It's not as if you did this to yourself."

No, I thought, I hadn't done it to myself, but whatever had happened had passed the realm of dreams or brain leaks or whatever the medical profession might call it. And crazy people don't wake up with a sunburn in a swimsuit they hadn't seen in 12 years. The swimsuit and the sunburn were the major clues. The response from Rick that he had dumped Lucy at my suggestion was another.

Dreamville, as I had been calling it, suddenly became a real place. Maybe the past. Maybe Rod Serling's "other dimension of sight and sound." But it was not my mind. Physical items did not come with you from dreams and I had physical evidence in the form of a neon pink bikini.

"Mr. Stewart," I said.

"Gordon, remember yesterday when you informed me your name was Pamela?"

Now he was making fun at my expense. I supposed I deserved that.

"Ok, ok. Call me April and I'll call you Gordon. Ok?"

He smiled and sat back down in the chair.

"Yes, April, what can I do for you?"

"Gordon," I said and paused. I didn't want to sound bitchy or arrogant.

"Rick said that we knew one another in high school. I'm sorry, but I don't remember you. I know I should, but, and I'm not trying to be rude, I really don't."

He laughed again.

"Now I'm truly shocked," he said.

"I doubt if you would have remembered me, although we were in the same homeroom. I was a new kid, only there for about two years, and you were, well, you traveled in a different crowd. I was the skinny kid with an accent and no history with you."

I felt like a jerk. If I ever went back to Dreamville, I was definitely going to look for him.

"I'm sorry. Really. I've always had a tendency to say what I think and ignore anything I . . ." I stopped, realizing how arrogant I sounded.

"Oh hell, I can't even get this apology out without sounding . . ."

"Forget it. It was ages ago. I assume we've both changed a bit since then," he said.

Well, he was right about part of that. He had certainly changed. He had changed so much that I didn't recognize him. But he seemed to remember everything about me. I had never thought of myself as a popular person in school, but I had enjoyed high school. I enjoyed class, my family and friends, and even then I had had a sarcastic streak that, while wasn't mean, could be sharp. The only thing that hadn't been great then had been being almost 6 feet tall. Oh, it helped in everything except experiences with the opposite sex. Teen age boys tend to shy away from tall girls, especially if the girls were smart and used sarcasm as pre-emptive strikes.

I had used that as my turtle shell long before I had met Vince and he had dumped me. I think I saw what damage could be done and I had kept them at arm's length on purpose. But I could also remember that I had never been asked out on a date the entire time I was in high school except by boys who were out of school and those boys were off limits by way of parental fiat.

Sometimes being a smart-ass did not have its rewards.

"Gordon, thank you again. I wish I could remember what happened last night. Maybe the police will find something."

I was getting good at lying. I knew exactly where I had been and what had happened and if I told even one person about Dreamville, as I was coming to call my nightly visits to the past, I knew that I would be locked up with 50 shrinks trying to diagnose some mental disorder or another. I wasn't going to tell anyone. Maybe the trips would stop. At least I would try to make sure that I was safe in a bed the next time I fell asleep in Dreamville.

Gordon stood to leave and paused at the curtain.

"It's ok that you didn't see me. But I saw you and I'm glad to see you now," he said and left.

How could I not have seen him? What a fool I had been.

Chapter Seven

Detective Maria Sullivan came in after Gordon left. She was followed by her partner, Dan Clarke, who stood next to her shaking snow off his coat and pulling off his ski cap. He was a big bear of a man. Hair everywhere except his face. He looked a little overweight, but I thought that most of it was probably muscle.

I waited for one them to speak and watched as Maria looked up to Detective Dan and whisper "Tu Madre" under her breath as she sat in the seat next to my bed. She pulled out a file and a laptop from her bag. She did not look like a very happy woman.

Her attitude irritated me and I snorted slightly and looked away from her. She was irritated? She should be in my position. I would much rather be anywhere but in this ER.

I suppose that she had noticed my anger and tried to ease the situation by apologizing, talking about the stack of manila folders on her desk, that her case load grew every day and every day it seemed as if nothing changed. She said that the victims couldn't, or wouldn't, remember, or that the forensic evidence was usually non existent or the perp wasn't in the system. She didn't really seem apologetic, but rather complaining about having to do her job.

"I'm so sorry that victims are such an inconvenience to you," I said tersely.

Detective Dan covered his mouth and I could tell he was stifling a smile behind that large hand. Obviously, he hadn't always enjoyed his partner's attitude, either.

She pulled at the neck of maroon turtleneck sweater she was wearing and leaned back in the chair, crossing her legs. She ignored my comment and I thought that maybe she was wishing she were home taking a hot soak in her tub or waiting for her husband or lover to arrive home, anything but being here and having to talk to me.

She surprised me by apologizing again. She began to talk about having to work in her unit, that it was making her crazy. Too many victims and a low clearance rate. The women are always so afraid that most of the time they never talk. They're always so ashamed or afraid that they rarely think about the next woman the son of a bitch who had hurt them would hurt.

"I feel useless sometimes, but I suppose that's no excuse," she said, but she still did not sound very sincere.

Once again, Detective Dan's hand went to his face, but this time to rub his temples. He appeared embarrassed by his partner's behavior. He reached inside his blazer and pulled out a jump drive to give to her.

"Maybe this'll help you remember something," he said to me. "Seems like the surveillance cameras had something to tell us."

She put the jump drive in her laptop and shook her head.

"I don't know, anything would help at this point. The rape kit came back negative, which is good for you. At least you weren't . . . you weren't abused."

As she typed on the laptop, she continued to speak..

"The docs have no explanation for a sunburn on one side of your body unless you were in a tanning bed that malfunctioned."

I rolled my eyes. This was getting so tiresome.

"How many times do I have to tell everyone that I have never used a tanning bed or a spray tan or any sort of self tanning lotion. Is anyone listening to me?"

Detective Dan pointed his finger at the screen as the recording began to play.

"Something happened last night and if you can explain it to us, it might help," he said to me.

Maria put the laptop on the bed and hit the play button. She leaned forward to watch the surveillance footage of my hallway as well as to watch my reactions.

"The first part is from two nights ago. I've fast forwarded to about 1 a.m. Watch," she said.

When the red time code came to 1:14 a.m., a woman suddenly appeared outside of my door, the same woman who had appeared in my bedroom in Dreamville. I gasped involuntarily and felt faint.

Chapter Eight

"Are you okay," Detective Dan said and asked if I needed a drink of water. He instructed Maria to stop the playback for a moment. The female detective did not look happy with his order, but she did what he said.

By that time I had recovered from the shock of seeing the woman from Dreamville outside of my apartment. If I were confused before, now I was completely baffled by what was on the surveillance recording.

"No," I said. "I'm ok. I just don't know who that woman is. I've never seen her in my building before."

The female detective looked up at her partner and sniffed as if she didn't believe a word I had said.

"Okay, then watch," she said.

I watched as the woman went into my apartment.

"Now I'm going to fast forward to around 9:30 a.m."

The woman was there again, standing outside my door and then was gone just as quickly.

Maria stopped it and looked at Dan and then at me.

"What the hell?" I asked. "That makes no sense. Has this thing been messed with? It looked like she just appeared and then disappeared."

Detective Dan was nodding his head. "Yeah, but the weirdness doesn't stop there. Fast forward, Maria."

She fast forwarded until I saw Gordon Stewart coming down the hall and she slowed the recording to real time. He walked up to my door and knocked, waited, and then the door opened and he entered the apartment.

"Fast forward again," Detective Dan said. "He's only there about 20 minutes."

"I know," I said. "I remember his visit."

Maria hit the forward button until she saw Stewart leaving. He seemed to be saying something and was smiling as he nodded good-bye. He walked away and down the hall and was smiling. Seeing the smile on his face made me smile for a brief second, but just as he disappeared from the camera's view, the woman from the previous night was there again, standing with her back to the camera. She was there for about three seconds and then was gone.

Maria paused the recording and looked at Dan.

"Is this some kind of joke," I asked. "Are you guys trying to have a big joke at my expense?"

Maria pushed the fast forward button and said, "No, seriously, this came straight from the apartment building surveillance cameras. Now watch."

She stopped the playback to real time just before 1:14 a.m. And there the woman was again. It looked as if she entered the apartment, but I didn't see the door open.

I was shaking my head. This was unreal. I was unaware of the fact that I was crying. This scared me and somewhere in my head something felt as if someone was trying to tell me something.

The detective fast forwarded again to around 9:30 a.m. and there the woman was again and then she wasn't. She then moved it forward to the doorman and Gordon pounding on my door. I watched as Frank used his pass key and they entered my apartment.

The rest of the playback was filled with the EMTs arriving and taking me from the apartment on a gurney. Then it stopped.

I wiped the tears from my face and looked away from them. They gave me a few seconds for me to try and compose myself

"I don't understand any of this. Who is that woman? Is this really from my hallway? It just makes no sense," I said.

Detective Dan shrugged his shoulders and looked at the floor.

"We don't know what this tape is about. It doesn't make any sense to use either. I mean it makes it you look like you're lying about something or that woman attacked you," Maria said.

"I am not lying."

I was royally pissed at her attitude and I had had enough of it.

"If you don't believe me and you're going to continue to insinuate these things, then I have nothing more to say to you. As a matter of fact, you should probably talk to my lawyer from now on."

Detective Dan stepped forward and pulled the laptop away and almost threw it at his partner.

"Ms. Norris, I am really sorry about this. We, I, believe you. We're just trying to make sense of it, too. I mean, you saw what we saw. We can't explain it and we hoped either you could or maybe it might jog your memory, cause, to tell you the truth, this is way above my pay grade. I'm really sorry we put you through this."

"Oh, and for the record," he went on, "We know you don't own a tanning bed and haven't ever used the one at your gym, or anywhere in your neighborhood."

Maria put the laptop and her things back into her bag.

"Listen," she said. "Either we're missing it, or that woman just appears and disappears from nowhere. And we've watched it again and again, especially last night's recording. It looks like the woman didn't have a key or that she even touched the doorknob. It's like she, ah hell, no. I'm not even going to say it."

Detective Dan raised his eyebrows. He leaned back against the wall.

"You don't have to," he said. "We know what you're thinking. It looks like she walked through the door itself."

Maria looked away from me and stared at the IV dripping. I knew from watching the expressions passing across her face that she, too, couldn't understand what she had seen.

"We're going to have the lab go over this and see if their computer guy can tell if anything's been done to it. I sure as hell have no idea what to write in a report based on the tape," she said.

Detective Dan was putting the jump drive back into his jacket pocket.

"Well, we're sorry that's all we've been able to find out, but if you remember anything, even the smallest detail, let us know. And again, I apologize. You're right. You're the victim, not the suspect and no one should treat you otherwise," he said, glancing down at his partner as she rose to leave with him.

"Me, too," she replied. "Me, too." But she didn't look sympathetic in any way. She looked tired and disgusted with the whole afternoon.

Chapter Nine

Rick and Lisa took me back to my apartment later that evening after the detectives had left. The doctor gave me a prescription for an ointment for the burn, told me when to return to have the stitches removed and basically told me that otherwise I was fine.

I wondered how "fine" they would think I was if they knew that everything that had happened to me had happened in Dreamville.

Strait-jacket for one, please. No one would believe me in a million years. This wasn't a sci-fi movie. It was my life. I just needed to figure two things – how it was happening and how to stop it.

Rick didn't want to leave me there alone, but Lisa, who was missing David in only the desperate way a new mother could, was ready to leave me to whatever fates would come. That almost pissed me off, but I knew her motherly instincts were stronger than any bonds of friendship or familial duties she might feel toward me. And that was as it should be.

So I scooted them out the door, promising to lock everything up after they left and try to just get some rest. Of course, this was after Rick had checked the locks on every window and door to the place, including the sliding doors to the small balcony where snow had piled against the door making it obvious to anyone who looked that no one had been out there.

I took a long shower and examined the cut on my cheek. Lovely. I wondered if I would I have to see someone about a scar if one remained, though it did look like the doctor had done of good job of stitching me up.

I put on a pair of silk boxers and a thin cotton t-shirt as clothing irritated my skin, grabbed my Kindle, and crawled into the bed. I had turned the heat up more than my frugal nature was happy with, but still felt chilled from the hot skin on the front of my body.

Just as I had begun to read a history of American glass making in the US, my house phone rang. I started not to answer it. I was really tired, but I was afraid it might be Rick coming back so I went to the phone and said "Yes," with just a little exasperated tone to my voice. My doorman informed me that Mr. Stewart was downstairs and would like to come up.

What time was it, I thought. This man was so unpredictable and he did frighten me just a little because I knew, absolutely knew, that had it not been for Dreamville, I would never have known him. In the world I had really lived as a teenager, he had not existed, at least not in my "real" world. I had never seen him in my life until the night we had all eaten dinner at Benito's in Little Italy. And after that dinner, he somehow he appeared in that first trip to Dreamville. Now he seemed to be everywhere.

"Send him up." I was hoping for a short visit and that this was just a wellness check on his part. I did not feel like entertaining, and that included cooking, drinking or even talking.

Several minutes later I was opening the door to him and his incredible stormy eyes.

"Come on in, though you'll have to excuse me if I'm not a great hostess. I had just climbed into bed with a book."

He smiled and immediately removed his coat. Now what part of the implied "please go home" did he not understand? I sighed and waved him into the living room where I slumped into my sofa.

"I've been worried about you since this afternoon," he said.

"I keep thinking that someone is stalking you. I thought maybe if I came over for a while it might drive them away."

The only stalker is starting to look like you, I thought, but didn't say it. I tried to assure him that I was fine, that Rick had checked the entire place from stem to stern and that the doorman was watching the place as if I were the Queen of Tonga.

He laughed at that, but still made no movements to indicate that he was going to leave.

"Really, Gordon, it's ok. You don't have to worry."

"It's no bother and my evening is free. Have you eaten? I can make a fantastic omelet. Something I learned when my parents lived here in the states. Let me fix you something," he said and headed into the kitchen.

I rolled my eyes and looked up. Good heavens, did this man not understand that I wanted to be alone? I sat on the sofa and heard him opening cabinet doors in the kitchen and sighed. No, he was not going to go away. I rose from the sofa and followed him into the kitchen.

Surprisingly, he had found everything he needed to cook an omelet. I sat on the stool at the island and rested my head against my hands. My cheek was throbbing and my poor skin was beginning to burn again. Please, go home, I silently begged and he looked up from the stove and smiled at me, then furrowed his brow.

He removed the pan from the stove and walked over to where I sat, gently took my elbow in his hand and led me towards my bedroom. He pulled the sheet and quilt back for me and plumped two pillows to place behind my head.

I was too tired and in too much pain to speak. He disappeared for a moment and reappeared with a glass of ginger ale and some ibuprophen. "Take these and stay here. I'll bring you your food. You still look too weak to be sitting up with me. Trust me. Okay?"

I nodded and took the ginger ale and pills from him. It was just too difficult to fight him on this. If he wanted to be here, he wasn't going to hear anything from me. I closed my eyes and waited for the pills to dull the throbbing.

It seemed as if only a few minutes had passed when he was suddenly back with a tray with the omelet, toast, and a fresh glass of ginger ale. Somehow he had even managed to locate my linen napkins. I scooted up on the bed into a better sitting position and winced from the sunburn.

I didn't think I was hungry, but his omelet was fantastic, just as he had described it. By the time I had finished it and the toast, my head had ceased the drumming thump-thump and for the first time that day I felt better.

He had left the room while I was eating and I could hear him in the kitchen. It sounded as if he were cleaning up. I put the tray on my nightstand and suddenly felt so tired. I lay my head on the pillow and fell asleep. I didn't see or hear him enter the bedroom and take the tray back to the kitchen. I just slept. No dreams that night, just peaceful rest.

I woke the next morning and felt much better, although my skin was still tender. I wondered when he had left. He had been kind to me last night. It had been nice to have someone there to take care of me.

As I threw on my silk robe, I walked through the apartment and to my surprise found him sound asleep on my couch, the TV on ESPN with the sound off. I smiled as I looked down at his sleeping face. There was no way that I would ever have forgotten that face, no matter how young it might have been when I first saw him.

And that made me realize that something had happened in Dreamville to bring him into my life so early and then back into my life now. Until I had first travelled to Dreamville he had simply not existed. I don't know how I knew that, but I did.

He must have sensed my presence in the room and he opened his eyes and slowly sat up on the sofa.

"Sorry. I meant to stay awake, but I fell asleep."

I shook my head at that. "No, good heavens, you didn't have to stay awake or even stay here. You should have gone home when I fell asleep myself."

He stretched his arms behind his neck and out.

"You'll think this is strange, but I felt that if I didn't stay, something might happen to you again."

Now he shook his head.

"I suppose that sounded very ridiculous. I must have been tired as well."

"It's okay," I said and sat down on the sofa next to him.

"I appreciate your concern, especially your 'fantastic' omelet. It was delicious."

He laughed at that and stood to get his coat.

"I'm going to head home. I think you'll be ok. And maybe tomorrow, we can go to your shop to look for furnishings for my flat."

"Absolutely," I said as I walked him to the door.

Just as he opened it, he turned back and stared into my eyes. I thought for a brief moment that he was going to kiss me, but he turned and walked down the hall to the elevator.

As I closed the door, I thought about that moment at the door. I had wanted him to kiss me. I had wanted it in the worst way. I leaned against the door and looked out into the apartment. Not a thing was out of place. It was as if he had never been there. That made me sad for some reason. No matter where he had come from, the lack of his presence changed my mood. I felt cold and went back through the bedroom to take a shower and try to wash the chlorine smell from hair.

How could I smell it and no one else had noticed it?

For a moment I thought I heard him back in the living room and walked back there.

"Did you forget . . ." I stopped mid-sentence. No one was there. I could have sworn I heard someone in there. I looked down and saw that the television was no longer on. I couldn't remember if either of us had turned it off when he left.

I shrugged my shoulders and headed back to the bathroom. And that was when I screamed. The woman from Dreamville was standing in my bathroom as if she were waiting for me.

Chapter Ten

I don't remember the last time I had run so fast. I ran from the apartment to the elevator, pushing the button over and over, the whole time watching the door of my apartment for the woman to appear. As the elevator arrived, I jumped into the car and pushed the lobby button and then the doors close button as well. Just as the doors were almost closed I saw her outside the elevator door.

I backed into the corner of the car and grabbed the wooden railing, terrified that somehow she had followed me into the elevator. When the doors opened onto the lobby, I ran to the doorman and told him that someone had broken into my apartment. He picked up the phone and dialed 911, informed the police of the break-in and then hung up.

"Sit down here, Ms. Norris. The police are on their way. No one can hurt you here."

I sat down in his chair and looked at the bank of monitors for the building. The monitors. Surely they had to record the interior of the building for certain periods of time. Maybe the woman was on the recording.

"Frank, the cameras in the building – do they record what goes on in the public areas?"

He hesitated for a second and then nodded.

"Can you bring up the recording for last night and this morning for me? I want to see how she got into my apartment."

Frank looked at me quizzically for a moment.

"A woman broke in?"

I nodded as he pulled up the footage for last night and this morning. What I didn't know was that he had already seen the woman on the recordings he had given the police.

"Frank, what's wrong?"

He shook his head. "The police told me not to say anything yesterday when they took the information from the last three weeks, but I saw a woman outside your apartment on the recordings they took."

I wanted to shrink into the chair and disappear. What he was saying was impossible.

"Frank, are you saying she's been there the past three weeks? Why didn't anyone tell me?"

I was furious. The police should have told me this. I shouldn't have had to find this strange woman in my apartment if they knew she had been stalking me.

Then I stopped to think about it. If I had seen her in Dreamville, how had I seen her here? Did I bring her here the way I had brought the pink bikini and sunburn from the past? Was she the thing on the third floor of my childhood home that I had feared so much? If she was, how had she come back with me?

Or was she from the real world? Was she stalking me, and if she was, why me?

My god, I thought, I am going crazy. Dreamville. The real world. I sounded like a lunatic in my own head. There had to be a rational explanation. Maybe none of this was real. Maybe I was in a coma and nothing was real. Maybe I was in hell.

"Ms. Norris, Ms. Norris . . ."

Frank was touching my shoulder and I looked up at him.

I was unaware that I was shaking. I was more terrified now than I had been when I had seen her in either Dreamville or the real world.

"Here's the playback," he said.

"How do I control the speed?"

"Use the mouse or the playback arrows on the keyboard," he said.

The recording started with Rick and Lisa bringing me home from the hospital. I fast forwarded to them leaving. Then I came to Gordon Stewart appearing outside my door. Nothing the rest of the night. Not a soul in the hallway, not even my neighbors.

"Frank, are the McKinleys in town?"

"No, Ms. Norris," he said. They're in London for the next two months. You're the only one on your floor. The other apartment is being renovated and Mrs. Cohn's apartment won't be cleared until the estate is settled. It's sealed until then. The locks were changed and no one's been there for the past few months."

"Is someone staying in the McKinleys' apartment or have you seen anyone else on the floor?"

He shook his head. "No, I'm holding their mail and papers for them in my office. I'd know if someone were staying there, but I do have numbers where I can reach them. I could call them and find out if they gave a key to someone who might have come into the building through the garage."

"That would be wonderful, Frank," but as I spoke, I saw Gordon Stewart leaving my apartment and entering the elevator. And that was when the terror returned.

"Frank, look!"

I turned the recording back to Stewart getting on the elevator. Just as the elevator closed, the woman was standing outside my apartment door. Unconsciously, I had grasped his arm and was squeezing it as I moved back from the monitor.

The woman did not open the door. One second she was there and the next time she was gone. And of course I knew where. She had somehow moved from my hallway to my bathroom. Seconds later, I came flying out of my apartment, my mouth open in a silent scream as I watched myself pushing the elevator button again and then jumping into the car.

I disappeared into the elevator and just as the security camera captured the door closing, it also captured the woman walking back down the hall away from the camera.

"Jesus Christ," I said and began to cry. "What in the name of heaven is going on?"

Frank knelt down and let me lean on his shoulder as I cried.

"It'll be okay, Ms. Norris. We'll get her. Don't worry. Don't cry. It's going to be okay."

But somehow, I was afraid nothing was ever going to be the same again.

I had brought my worst childhood fear from Dreamville into my world. And I was scared that this time, she was not going to let me get away.

The police arrived just as I had finished watching the playback. They were followed by the female Detective from the hospital yesterday and giant of a man, Detective Dan.

They watched the recording. The woman detective instructed the policemen in uniform to go up the stairs and she and her partner would take the elevator.

I was still clutching Frank's arm as they left to go to my floor. I knew they would find nothing. The thing – the woman – she wouldn't be there for them to find. That would explain why I hadn't seen her last night. Stewart had been there. She wasn't going to be there unless I was there alone.

"Frank, can I use your phone?"

He replied, "Of course," and handed me the receiver to the house phone. I dialed my brother's house first and tried not to let him hear the fear in my voice. I asked him for Gordon Stewart's number and gave him a story that I had misplaced it.

It was going into voice mail when Stewart answered it, his voice hoarse. I explained what had just happened and he said he'd be there in five minutes, not to move.

No chance of that, I thought, and realized that I needed to let go of Frank's arm. I tried to compose myself, but between the experience and my sudden awareness that I was wearing little but a thin yellow silk robe, I was starting to feel very embarrassed.

Gordon Stewart arrived just as the detectives came back down from the apartment. We all watched the recording again, then the detectives took a jump drive out and copied the recording to it.

Gordon and Frank stood behind me and now Gordon was clasping my right hand in his. He looked confused and angry while Frank simply looked as scared as I felt.

"What the hell is going on here?" Gordon asked the detectives.

The female detective looked to Detective Dan, and then to us.

"Frankly, we don't know. We've found this woman in the playbacks for the last three weeks of Ms. Norris's floor. But she never faces the camera so we can't get a look at her. And . . . well, you just saw what happens. One second she's there, the next she's not."

"We've got out computer people on this," Detective Dan said.

"And maybe they'll get something off of it that we've missed."

He didn't sound very convinced and the female detective raised one eyebrow when he finished speaking.

Gordon saw that small gesture and moved closer to them.

"Listen, you can raise your eyebrows all you want, but this woman is being stalked and if your department doesn't want to help, I know someone who will."

She turned to face him with a grim look on her face.

"Oh you do, and who exactly are you and how are you involved in this?"

When Gordon said his name, her demeanor became a bit more subdued and her partner actually backed away from Gordon a few steps. Their attitude toward him and what was happening completely changed.

"Sir, we are taking this quite seriously. We'll keep you both informed. I promise," she said, this time without the attitude or the raised eyebrow.

Gordon gazed at me and saw that I was still in my robe.

"April, I'll go get you something to wear from upstairs. I'm still not convinced that it's safe for you to return," he said.

"That would be great. I have no desire to go back up there."

"Gordon," I said, "Could you grab my purse off my sofa table, too?"

He smiled and went upstairs to retrieve my clothing and purse. As the elevator left, I overheard Detective Dan say something to his partner about Gordon and he was gesturing animatedly as he spoke. His partner was shaking her head as he spoke.

"What are you two talking about? What did you say about Mr. Stewart?"

Detective Dan's shoulders fell and he walked back over to the desk where I still sat.

"We didn't know that Mr. Stewart was a friend of yours. We didn't recognize him from the playback."

"What the hell are you talking about?"

The female detective walked over to us.

"You mean you don't know?" she asked.

"Know what? You people are making me crazier than that woman. What's going on?"

"Your friend, Mr. Stewart, has, well, has friends. Wealthy and influential man."

I'm sure my jaw dropped open at that point. I had no idea what they were talking about.

"Wait, what are you saying?"

The female detective sighed as if she were wondering how this particular shit storm had landed on her doorstep.

"Ms. Norris, we're not giving anyone preferential treatment, but some people have enough influence to push. Let's just leave it at that. Anyway, his involvement moves this to major crimes, so you'll probably have new detectives assigned to your case."

"No, no. I don't want that," I said. "You two have been here from the beginning. I don't want to start over with someone else. I trust the two of you to find this woman. I'll talk to Mr. Stewart. This is about me, not him. Okay?"

Detective Dan looked to his unhappy partner and shrugged.

"If that's what you want, you've got it," he said. "But please be patient. We're trying as hard as we can to figure out how this woman's getting into the building."

The female detective reached out her hand and placed it on my shoulder.

"We really are trying to help you, but your friend is probably concerned that he's not getting the best help for you. My husband would probably be the same way."

"Mr. Stewart is neither my husband nor involved with me beyond business. I apologize to you both for his rudeness. It won't happen again."

She smiled and she and Detective Dan headed towards the stairwell to the garage. She paused before she left and looked at me.

"No matter what your relationship is with him, I agree with him about one thing. I would not go back to the apartment. In fact, I would go somewhere that no one knows about."

"I can't do that," I said. "I have a business and employees who depend on me. I can't just leave everything."

Before she could object, I continued.

"But I can stay somewhere else that no one would know about. Would that help?"

"It's better than staying here," she said and followed Detective Dan into the stairwell.

To say that I was angry with both Gordon Stewart and my brother Rick was putting it mildly.

I was seething by the time Stewart returned with my clothing. He saw the anger in my face.

"They told you, didn't they?"

"Yes," I said tersely.

"Why didn't you? And asking me to help you furnish a flat? You probably own several here already. I feel like a fool. Either you or Rick should have told me."

He held out my clothing to me.

"I didn't want it to make a difference. I wanted to know you as the girl I knew in high school, the one with the sharp tongue, who always had a book in her hand. I'm sorry. Truly."

I jerked my clothes from him.

"I didn't have a sharp tongue," I mumbled.

He laughed out loud.

"No, of course you didn't – the girl who called our homeroom teacher a "Chair Nazi.""

I realized that that had not really happened except in Dreamville and I froze. Dreamville wasn't just my dreams. It was my past. And I had changed it. No one would know what he had just said unless I had gone back and actually done it. Dreamville was real.

Chapter Eleven

A town car was waiting outside my building when Stewart and I left. I noticed that Stewart had generously tipped Frank as we left and entered the car.

"Where to now, princess?"

I snorted. How dare he say that to me? I hadn't lied.

"Don't call me that. I'm not the entitled one in this car."

"It's what Rick and I called you in high school, don't you remember? The summer before Rick left for Maryland and we all hung out at your pool? I wasn't being condescending."

He sounded puzzled by my response. Had I spent an entire summer with this man and my brother? Obviously my trip to Dreamville had made it happen. So why didn't I remember it. All I remembered was the way things really happened – a summer spent by the pool mooning over a broken heart and reading everything I could get my hands on. I had stayed away from everyone that summer. I was so embarrassed by being dumped by Vince that I didn't want to face any of my friends from school.

That was what really happened that summer. That was what I remembered. I know that I did not spend the summer with Stewart and my brother. The supposed house that Stewart's family had occupied did not exist. It was a large wooded tract of land where my brothers and I had played as children. At one time, there had been some talk of building a pool there, but nothing came of it. Nothing was there. Not the Stewarts and not their house.

But somehow my first trip to Dreamville had changed that. Was it seeing Gordon in the hall in that first dream that had started the chain of events that led me to sitting next to him in this town car with a history that had never happened?

"If you don't mind, I thought I'd take you to my flat. I have plenty of room and you could help me with the project while you stayed there," he said.

Well, that would be great except that I had no clothes and I doubted that he really needed my help in furnishing his "flat". I was still a little angry over his failure to give me full disclosure on whom he was. But then, wasn't I keeping my own secrets?

We arrived at his "flat", which turned out to be the entire floor of a building on the upper east side. He actually had a place overlooking the park. Why in the world had he contacted me, or Rick for that matter, when he obviously could afford more expensive firms to assist him?

The apartment was spartan, to put it mildly. One sofa, a few chairs and a table, and only two beds in the bedrooms. He hadn't been joking when he said he needed to furnish the place.

"Great place, but I think you need some furniture. Why didn't you bring things over? I assume you could afford to do so?"

He walked over to the French doors leading to a large open terrace overlooking the park.

"I thought I'd find things here. What I have in Scotland stays there. Part of the legacy."

"Ah," I said. "But what about when you return home? You'll have a furnished place here that you might not be able to move in this real estate market."

He turned back to face me from the doors and smiled.

"I don't plan on giving up this place. I'll have my home there and a home here. My business involves both sides of the pond, so to speak. I just hope your brother doesn't mind the occasional trip to Scotland or Europe."

It was my turn to frown.

"What exactly do you do, besides being "influential" and wealthy? Are you some sort of Earl or squire or whatever the hell you people call yourselves?" And then I giggled. I couldn't help it. All I could think of was the song "Duke of Earl."

He sat down on the sofa and raised his eyebrows at my giggles.

"Are you sure you're feeling okay?"

I nodded, but started to laugh out loud now. The stupid song would not leave my brain. Maybe it was my mind's only defense against the past few days.

I fell into one of his few chairs and tried to compose myself, but every time he started to speak, the refrain from that song would start up again.

I took a deep breath and tried to become serious.

"I'm sorry. It's been a long week."

He leaned back against the sofa and stretched his arms along the back of the top of it. It was truly a horrible sofa and the ugliest color of hospital green I had seen in a long time.

"That is one truly ugly sofa," I said and began to giggle again, hoping to change the subject.

"I have several import/export businesses which specialize in Scottish and American items. All strictly legal, mind you, and the factories I own employ numerous people in both Scotland and America."

Okay, so he was a legitimate businessman. That was one less worry for myself, but especially for my brother. The last thing Rick needed now was to get involved in some shady enterprise. But, if Stewart was the friend he said he had been when we were younger, then surely he wouldn't use Rick as a patsy? My suspicions were raised again and I unconsciously frowned.

He ignored the frown and waved one hand out toward the apartment.

"As you can see, the flat is unfurnished and undecorated. I'd like it to have a comfortable home feel, but still have it look sophisticated enough to use to entertain clients and guests. I suppose what I saying is that I want a home, but one that reflects my Scottish roots and my American home. Does that make sense?"

"Yes, of course. You want a traditional feel using antiques that aren't ostentatious, yet have a "luxe" feel to them. Does that sound right?"

"Absolutely. That sounds fantastic. When can you start? You can stay in the one guest room while you work until this mess with your apartment is straightened out. That is if you'd like. I don't think your stalker will be able to find you here."

I sighed. My stalker. I didn't even know if she was real. Hell, I was still trying to accept that the man sitting across from me was really someone I used to know.

"Well, I need someone to get my clothing and some other things from my apartment. I guess I could always go back there and . . ."

He interrupted me. "No. That would not be a very wise idea. I have someone who could make the arrangements for you. I'll get her on the phone and you can tell her where everything you need will be."

I shook my head. The thought of a stranger in my home bothered me a great deal and I was already too indebted to this man as it was.

"I don't want you to put someone else in possible danger, especially if she already have her own job tasks to perform."

He leaned forward and pulled out his iPhone from his jacket pocket.

"Not a problem. I'll send my driver with her. They can bring your things here. She'll be perfectly safe."

I tried to object again, but saw that he was determined.

Before I knew it, he was handing me the phone and introducing me to Helen, his personal assistant, who would see to the tasks that needed to be done. I gave her the instructions on what I would need for a few weeks, not really knowing how long this "protection period" was.

While I talked with Helen, Stewart had gone into the kitchen and had begun to make sandwiches. I was amazed at the size of the kitchen. A small party could be catered from within it.

"How big is this place?"

He shrugged. He didn't seem to care about the size.

"It's small compared to my house in Scotland. I don't know. Four or five bedrooms, maybe. I have the entire place to myself. Do you like ham or turkey?

"Both," I said and began to open cabinet doors in the kitchen. The cabinets were empty except for a few plates and glasses. Very few food items except for what was in the fridge and nothing else.

"You really haven't bought anything, have you?"

"No, didn't really know what would work best and I had a few other things to take care of. Juice, coffee, tea?"

"Juice is fine," I said and stood at the stainless steel counter and began to eat the sandwich he had made for me. I was ravenous and had finished my sandwich before he had barely started to eat his.

"Why don't you wander around the flat and get an idea of what you're going to need. There is an library which I'd like to use as an office for personal affairs, but the rest of the place is open for your interpretation."

I started out of the kitchen and stopped at the doorway and looked back to him.

"You're trusting an awful lot to someone you haven't seen in over a decade. How do you know I won't mess the entire project up?"

He laughed. "I did my research on your business first and I remembered your home. I felt your tastes were probably spot on what I needed."

"And my brother? He did have some market problems."

I gave him a very pointed look.

Stewart took a drink of milk and wiped his lip with a paper napkin.

"So did a lot of smart people. Rick is honest and loyal, both qualities sadly lacking in some brokers. The entire market mistakes were foisted on him by his old firm. I don't worry about that happening again."

I nodded and wandered away through his "flat". It was the size of a large house, rather than an apartment and I wondered just how much money he had to afford this place. It must have cost a fortune to buy and it would cost a small fortune to furnish it the way he wanted.

I ended up back in the living room area and looked around it closely.

I decided that I would start there first and the first thing I had to do was to get rid of that horrible sofa. The few armchairs could be used in other rooms. I felt like an artist staring at a blank canvas. I could empty my entire store and still not fill this flat. He needed everything, from china to carpets and art for the walls. Even the beds were simply mattresses and springs on frames and only his bedroom had a small bed table.

He came into the living room and opened the French doors and walked out onto the terrace. I followed him and saw a beautiful space, covered in snow. I stood at the door and mentioned that he'd need to think about doing something out there when the weather was warmer.

"So, you're willing to take this on?"

"I suppose, but I'm going to have to have your input on a lot of things and we need to sit down and work out a budget. You mentioned your business. Does it manufacture any items you might want to include."

He laughed. "If we're having guests, we might. Most of the items are food."

"You mean if 'you're having guests', I believe."

"Of course. Isn't that what I said?" he said and raised one eyebrow, but I could see amusement in his eyes.

"Will you stop calling me Mr. Stewart? Call me Gordon or Stew like you used to. Only my employees call me Mr. Stewart."

I sighed and picked up my purse as I headed for the foyer leading to the elevator.

"I am your employee, so to speak," I said and punched the down button hard.

"No, you're my friend. You and your brother are two of my oldest friends. I refuse to have either one of you address me as Mr. Stewart."

I mumbled "whatever" under my breath and entered the elevator with him. He was irritating as hell for someone who hadn't existed until I had gone to Dreamville.

It was then that I realized that I hadn't thought about the morning's events or Dreamville the entire time we had been at his apartment. I didn't know whether that was a good thing or a bad thing, but I somehow didn't think that my trips to Dreamville or my unwanted guest were done with me yet.

Chapter Twelve

By the time Gordon had finished charming the ladies at my store, we had tagged a truck load of items to be taken to his flat, mostly items that were needed just to live right now, including bed tables, lamps, and a complete set of Lenox dishes.

"We can find something else for your dinner parties, but you need the Lenox for any smaller gatherings. You're also going to have to hire a housekeeper. Those dishes and crystal do not go into any dishwasher."

"Not a problem. Can you contact an agency for me? Perhaps you could interview her in the next week or so.?"

I frowned again. How did I end up being his personal assistant as well as his decorator?

"Gordon, I'm more than happy to work for you on this project, but I do have other clients."

"Can't you do both? I mean, help me and still look for their items while we're furnishing my place?"

I cleared my throat and started to count before answering his question. He was not listening to me. I wondered if he had been this obtuse when he had been younger and then realized that I was supposed to know whether he had been. What a colossal mess!

"Gordon. Listen. I cannot hire people for you. I can give you a certain amount of my time, but that's it. You need a personnel director to hire people for housekeeping."

He turned to look at me at then out the window of the town car.

"Absolutely. You're absolutely right. I'll call Helen and have her set up some interviews for you."

I wanted to scream now. Was the man being intentionally dense?

I placed my hand on his arm and felt the soft camel hair coat he was wearing against my skin.

"Gordon. Listen to me, again. I cannot hire a housekeeper for you. I cannot interview potential employees for you. I have a business. You are my client. We have no contract. We both can terminate this arrangement at any time."

He furrowed his brow in that way that made me want to touch his face.

Damn it. Stop, I thought. Do not start caring about this man, I told myself.

"I just assumed that since you would be staying at the flat that you would want to assist in hiring staff."

"I'm not living with you. I'm staying with you temporarily which I'm starting to think is a stupid idea. Maybe I should stay at Rick and Lisa's," I said, though I knew that I couldn't do that. The commute into the city alone would take two hours out of my day, not to mention that I didn't want to endanger them.

Gordon took my hand from his arm and held it between his hands which were surprisingly rough for a man who hired people to work for him.

The texture of his skin was almost like an electric shock to my own hand and I tried to extricate myself from his hold.

"I'm sorry. I'm moving far too fast and I've forgotten that you have your own situations to sort out. But, if you think about it, it does make sense for you to interview the housekeeper. You wouldn't want just anyone handling the antiques."

Damn him. He had boxed me in. I had nowhere to hide from that question, no rhetoric with which to respond. He was correct. The housekeeper had to be aware of the nature of the items being chosen for his flat and had to know how to care for them properly. I pulled my hand from his and slid a little further from him on the seat.

"I suppose you're right about that. But, Helen has to vet the potential candidates before I interview anyone."

He smiled and punched a number into his ever present phone. I knew he was calling Helen.

"Ask her about my clothes. I'd prefer not to have to spend money on buying new clothes. Damn it, why can't you just go with me to get my things? Whomever the woman was, she didn't come around when you were there."

He held up his hand as he tried to talk to Helen and listen to my complaints at the same time.

"I see," he said. "Fantastic. Helen, you're priceless. Remind me to remember that come payday."

He laughed at something she said and then clicked off the phone.

"Everything's set. The first candidates should come by tomorrow afternoon. With the items being delivered tomorrow, you'll need help in getting the first things we've decided on unpacked."

"And what about my things?"

He patted my knee as if I were a child.

"Don't worry. Everything's in order. Are you hungry? Would you like to go by Benito's for supper?"

Of course, Gordon. Yes, Gordon. Whatever you say, Gordon. Arrgh! This man was not the boy I remembered from Dreamville. This man was infuriatingly efficient, taking everything as it came without thinking twice about anyone around him.

But instead of saying any of that, I merely nodded and watched as the car moved through Chinatown toward Mulberry Street.

After we arrived back at his apartment - I had decidedly that I would never call it a 'flat' again, I was feeling exhausted and knew that tomorrow would be a very busy day. I didn't bother to say good night, but just headed toward the guest room that was serving as my room for the time being.

As I turned on the light, I was stunned to find that all my clothing, toiletries, and personal items had not only been moved from my apartment, but were neatly placed in boxes marked with their contents and the clothing hung in the walk-in closet. Did he have Helen do this? Who moved my things? Who went through my drawers and handled my personal items?

I angrily strode into the living room and found him nowhere to be seen. I opened the terrace doors, but he was not out there and I quickly closed the doors against the freezing air.

"Gordon!" I yelled. Surely he could hear me in that cavernously empty apartment.

Finally I heard footsteps coming from his library.

He had run down the hall. Oh, shit. I shouldn't have yelled quite so loudly.

"Is something wrong? Are you ok?"

I decided to ignore his concern and address the invasion of my privacy.

"Yes, something is wrong. Who moved my things? I didn't want a stranger going through my drawers."

He relaxed his shoulders and turned to walk back to his office.

"Your sister-in-law packed for you while your brother was there as well as Frank, the doorman. Give me enough credit not to have strangers in your apartment."

I could feel my face turning an even deeper red than the sunburn had left it, but he never saw it. He was gone before I could respond. I sat down on the ugly hospital sofa and sighed. The only thing I could think to do was to go to bed.

I stopped outside the closed door of his library and started to knock, but held my hand back. I could tell him I was sorry, but in my own stubborn way, all I could do was head to my 'bed'.

I prayed that I would not visit Dreamville as I fell asleep.

Chapter Thirteen

Never pray for something not to happen that you know is destined to be.

I awoke in Dreamville the minute I fell asleep. I was in my bedroom again. Oh, hell. I had to go through the same routine again. Try to find out the date. Try to remember what was happening in my life at that time. This was getting so tiresome.

I opened the dresser drawers and found the pink swimsuit tucked in with my lingerie.

Well, that made no sense. The pink swimsuit was in the trash in 2012. Unless I had traveled to a time before I had worn it. I examined my arms and found the sunburn was completely gone. In fact, my skin was pale and the room was rather cold.

As I passed the radiator to open the drapes on the window, I felt heat emanating from it. Winter? It was winter? I should be at Columbia if it were winter. I threw open the drapes and saw snow everywhere. Surely it couldn't be . . .

My senior year of high school had been interrupted by the worst blizzard the state had seen in 30 years. I quickly dressed and ran downstairs. My entire family was sitting in the family room.

"You should have slept in," my father said as he pushed buttons on a large remote control. He was trying to find a channel. I looked down and saw the old Sony TV that we had had. The television was actually only a few years old then.

My mother was sitting next to my father's recliner in an armchair while my grandmother sat on the leather sofa and watched the snow falling outside.

"Gonna go with us up the hill?" Carl asked. He was referring to the bunny slope of a hill several blocks from the house where we all hung out on snow days.

Snow days. God, life was so free then. A snow day meant no worries about anything but avoiding snowballs and tumbling down the hill, holding onto the round plastic disc that seemed to fly.

I was 17 now. Two years younger. These travels to Dreamville made no sense. No order to them. One year I was 16, the next 19, and now 17.

What had happened in those years that kept me coming back here?

My grandmother spoke and started to get up from the sofa.

"You'll want to eat if you're going to be out all day."

"No, Grandma, I'm not going out now. I may go later. I can fix myself some cereal."

Rick threw a boot at me, which I swiftly dodged.

"Ha-ha. Really funny, April. C'mon guys. Let's get out of here and let the Princess be a jerk."

"Rick," my dad said in warning, but the boys left the family room and headed to the back door to finish putting on everything they needed for a day in the snow.

"April, get that ten dollar bill on top of the TV and give it to Rick. He forgot it and the boys will need it to get lunch," my mom directed.

Ten dollars? For lunch? I tried to think of where they'd get food for ten dollars and then I remembered the hot dog coach that always managed to make it to the hill no matter how much snow was on the road. Two hot dogs and a hot cocoa for two dollars. Dreamville had some advantages financially, I supposed as I walked through the house with the money.

I handed it to Rick and he grinned.

"I'll save you a dollar, if you want," he offered.

I shook my head. I remembered those hot dogs. They were only good because it was so cold by the time lunch rolled around. No, my nostalgia for items in Dreamville did not include those hot dogs.

I went into the kitchen where my grandmother had somehow followed me without my noticing and was preparing to fix my breakfast. She had pulled a round cardboard carton of Quaker Oats from the cabinet and was filling a pan with hot water.

"Grandma, I can fix my oats. You don't have to wait on me."

"Nonsense," she said. "You have to eat. Besides, I get bored sitting in there watching your father switch channels every five minutes."

I laughed.

"Yeah, he's always been a channel surfer."

"A what?" she asked.

Damn! I kept forgetting where I was.

"It's something the kids call people who change the channels a lot," I said.

She shook her head and continued with her cooking.

I walked back into the living room where the TV was now dark and my father was reading the paper that had to be from the day before. Ah! A chance to see when I had landed in Dreamville.

"Dad, could I see a section of the paper?"

"Sure," he said, reaching out part of it to me. "It's yesterday's edition. I don't think we're going to get one today and now it looks like the cable's out as well."

I grabbed the paper and threw myself on the sofa with the enthusiasm only a 17 year old could muster.

"April. The furniture. It's not for bouncing," my mother said.

January 8. The Superbowl was a few weeks away. I wondered if I were going to be there long enough to make a bet on the game. I remembered that game. Actually, I remembered more than a few of them. With three brothers, the Superbowl was a big deal around our house. Friends of my parents and brothers would be there and tons of snack food, soda, and beer.

Who would take a bet from me? Maybe I could go back to my real world with some money. That would certainly be interesting, waking with a wadful of cash in my hand or maybe tucked in my undies. One problem - I didn't have any money with which to make a bet.

Then I thought of Gordon. If I had changed the past on the first trip, then he should still be here for this trip. I could bet with him and he wouldn't make a big deal about asking to see the money. And, he would have plenty of money in the future so one bet couldn't make a difference, could it?

I pondered these paradoxes between Dreamville and my real world as I ate my oatmeal.

What if the bet changed things for Gordon?

Nonsense, I thought, hearing my grandmother's voice in my head.. His family was wealthy.

One small football wager wouldn't make a difference. I decided to get dressed and go in search of the skinny boy who would become the man I couldn't believe I had never noticed.

It would serve him right. Having my things moved without asking me.

Hiding his true identity from me. Who did he think he was?

By the time I had made it to the hill, I had gathered enough of what I thought of as righteous indignation at his actions. Then I saw him standing alone, watching the other kids flying down the hill. He looked so lonely. Hadn't he had any friends when we were in school? Just because I didn't remember him didn't mean that he hadn't impacted someone else's life, did it?

But still, there he was – alone and looking a little forlorn as I approached him.

When I called his name, I was surprised to see those familiar blue-gray eyes in such a young face. Suddenly I wanted to kiss him as much as I had in the real world.

He quickly turned away from me and started walking away from the hill.

"Hey, Gordon, wait. Where are you going?" I called.

He stopped, turned and looked at me with a small bit of disdain.

"If you're here to laugh at me, you can forget it. Hell can freeze over before I let you make me look foolish again," he said wit a stronger and more pronounced Scottish accent.

What the hell? What had I done since the first time I had been to Dreamville?

"Wait, Gordon. Listen. I'm sorry. Please," I said just as my feet flew out from under me on the icy sidewalk. I landed hard on my butt and felt my arm starting to throb where I had landed.

He turned just in time to see me fall and started to laugh as did several other kids in our class who had seen my feet fly up into the air.

I struggled to try to stand, but I couldn't get my left arm to push my weight up. Suddenly, I remembered breaking my arm my senior year, but I recalled it was from sledding into a fencepost and not from falling on a sidewalk.

If I remembered correctly, I had had to depend on my brothers to get me home, where by that time, my dad had managed to clear our drive and sidewalk.

But this time, I broke it chasing Gordon in order to con him into making a Superbowl bet. I lay back down on the sidewalk and looked up at the gray sky. I supposed I deserved it. I had been going to use the past to change things for me and to hurt him. Only fair that I suffer trying to make him hurt. Tears were forming in my eyes and I didn't know if it was from my shame at trying to trick him or from the pain in my arm.

When he saw me lay my head back down on the sidewalk, he stopped laughing and ran over to where I lay.

"Are you hurt?"

"Yes," I sighed. "I think I've broken my arm. Can you get my brothers?"

He looked up and then back to me.

"They're on their way here, now. Don't cry. It's going to be okay. Let me try to help you sit up," he said and lifted me up by gently placing his arms behind my back. I was sitting in frozen jeans by the time my brothers reached me.

"April, are you okay," David said.

"Get away from her, creep," Rick said to Gordon.

I used my right arm to push Rick away.

"Stop that, Rick. He was helping me. Don't be mean."

"My Jeep is right there. We can take her to the hospital. She says she thinks her arm is broken," Gordon said quietly.

My brothers and Gordon helped me to my feet and almost carried me to Gordon's Jeep and placed me in the front seat. Rick crawled behind me and told Carl and David to go home and tell our parents what had happened.

Gordon began to drive carefully down the snow covered street as Rick tried to direct him to the hospital.

"I know where it is. My father works there," he said and Rick became quiet for a moment.

"I'm sorry I called you a creep. I though you had pushed her down after what happened last week," Rick said.

Last week? Good god, what had I done to Gordon? Whatever it was, it was enough to make him walk away from me. Smooth move, April. Alienate the one person who's going to help you and your brother in the real world.

"Rick, he was helping me. Now, can you two stop it and get me to the hospital. My arm hurts like a son of a bitch."

Both boys stared at me.

Oh god, the 32 year old was talking again. I was about to give up. This business of trying to keep Dreamville and my real world straight was becoming impossible. I was 32 years old, not 17. I was tired of apologizing or making up stories about things I said or knew and my arm did hurt like a son of a bitch.

"Just fucking drive," I said and closed my eyes.

Neither boy said a word and for once I was thankful that no one was asking me questions about how I was acting.

By the time my parents had gotten to the hospital emergency room, the doctor had given me something for pain and I was starting to feel sleepy. Gordon and Rick were still there with me. As I began to doze off, I called them over to the bed.

"Gordon, thank you and I'm sorry if I was rude before and for what I did. Listen, both of you, the Rams are going to win Sunday. It's a sure thing. You and Rick . . ." I said and the room went dark.

Chapter Fourteen

I woke up in a dark room and was unsure as to whether I was still in Dreamville or back at Gordon's apartment. It was night and the room was pitch black. The bed felt bigger than a hospital bed, but it wasn't my bed in my apartment.

I was trying to get my eyes to adjust to the little bit of light in the room when I heard raspy breathing coming from the left corner of the room. Oh god, had the woman found me or followed me again?

I quietly tried to reach out to find a bed side lamp with my left hand and felt pain shoot up from my wrist to my shoulder and I screamed. The pain was unbearable. I rolled to my right reached out for a lamp on that side. This time I found the lamp. Just as I turned on the light, I looked to see a form fading back into the wall. Oh, god, she had found me. How? How? And what the hell was wrong with my left arm?

I was unaware of the tears falling as Gordon burst into the room. I cradled my left arm and thought I would pass out from the pain. What had I been doing in Dreamville this time? Broken arm. I had broken my arm and I had passed out before the doctors had set it.

"Are you okay, April?" he asked and moved swiftly to my bedside and took me in his arms and kissed my forehead.

Okay. I had changed something. This was not the same man who had offered me a place to stay. Who was this man? He looked something like the Gordon I had seen before I fell asleep, but he didn't act like him. What had I done?

"My arm. Jesus, it hurts," I said.

"I know. Remember the doctor said it would. Luckily it was just a hairline fracture of your elbow. You must have rolled over on it in your sleep. I'll get you something for the pain and a glass of water. Don't try to move," he said.

None of this made any sense. I looked to the corner of the room, but there was no shape there, no evidence that anyone or anything had been. And that was when I noticed that the room was completely furnished and decorated.

When I had gone to bed, there was nothing in the room but a bed and two bed tables with lamps from my shop. Now the room was painted a pale yellow and decorated with antiques and an impressionist painting on the wall that I swore looked like a Waterhouse.

How did my visit to Dreamville when I was 17 change all this? I hadn't even known Gordon Stewart a week and here I was in a bedroom I had obviously decorated and he had kissed my forehead.

He had kissed my forehead. I continued to cradle my left arm and that was when I noticed the large diamond ring on my left hand. What in the name of god was going on?

Before I could think any further, Gordon returned with a pill and the water. I took it and drank the water down. I was so thirsty. Then my stomach lurched as it did every time I returned from Dreamville and I though I was going to be ill.

Gordon must have seen the look on my face and he quickly lifted me up and carried me to the bathroom off from the bedroom.

The surprise of his quick movement brought me back into the real world and the nausea passed as quickly as it came. He saw the color returning to my face and smiled and this time kissed my lips lightly, which made me blush.

"C'mon. Doctor or no doctor, I'm putting you in our bed. You'll sleep better with me than in this guest room," he said.

Did he say 'our room'? I felt weak again, but I wanted him to put me down. Our room? Since when did we have an 'our room'?

"Gordon, put me down. I'm okay now. Please."

He lowered my feet to the ground and I realized that I was wearing one of his shirts and not much else. I had not gone to bed in that. I started to walk back to the bed and began to wobble and weave as I moved.

He quickly moved back to my right side and led me out into the hall and down the corridor. As we passed through the entry hall I saw a Hopper painting in the large entry hall. I decided I was hallucinating everything. This apartment had been completely empty when I had gone to bed. Now it was fully furnished and decorated.

I had to still be in Dreamville and was hallucinating about my real world because this was not my real world.

Gordon opened a door into what had been his bedroom, but now looked to be one that we shared together. He helped me into the bed and started to turn the light off.

"No! No, leave the light on," I said.

"Still having that nightmare? We've got to talk about this sometime. You can't continue to let this rule your life. It's been a year since the woman was seen. And we don't want to take this with us to Scotland next month."

A year? Scotland? I had lost a year? Oh my god, had my entire life become Dreamville? Had the real world ceased to exist at all? Maybe I was really sick. Maybe I was lying comatose in a hospital bed somewhere and this was all brain damage.

I began to cry again and he sat back down on the bed next to me and wiped the tears away from my eyes with his thumb.

"Don't cry, love. I'll stay here with you.."

He put his arm under me and pulled me closer to him. His every touch felt so right and so natural. I snuggled against his long body and felt the pain easing in my elbow.

But I had to know what had happened to change my life this much and I somehow thought that maybe he might be able to help me remember, especially if I had lost a year of my life somehow.

"Gordon, what's the date?"

"It's the 8th of January, love. Why?"

"No, the day. The painkiller is making my head feel fuzzy."

"It's January 8, 2002. You fell yesterday ice skating at Rockefeller Center. Cracked your elbow and hit your head fairly hard as well. Good thing, you're so hard headed," he laughed.

2002? I wasn't 32. I was 25. Oh my god, Dreamville had become my life. All the things that had led me to my 32nd birthday had not happened and might not happen. How could the future I knew happen if I was here in Gordon's arms now.

"Why are we going to Scotland, Gordon?" I was so confused.

"Don't we have work here?"

He smiled and tilted my head up to his and kissed me. Those little electric shocks were passing through my body again as he continued to kiss me.

"You really did hit your head. Our honeymoon, my love. You'll finally get to visit the drafty old house I grew up in before my father took the fellowship at Columbia Presbyterian."

"Fellowship? Gordon, I thought your father was a businessman? Why is he at Columbia Presbyterian."

"You really did hit your head yesterday. April, my father's a doctor. Always has been."

"So what do you do, Gordon? Seriously, what is your profession?"

"I'm with the diplomatic corps, April. I started there when I finished university, about the same time you were finishing your master's degree in biology."

Amazement. Confusion. Fear. Everything roiled to the surface. I couldn't remember anything and everything I had thought was right was wrong. Nothing was familiar except for his arms around me. Why me?

My mind was so fuzzy. I tried to think straight, but the pills had started jumbling everything into one awful nightmare. I starting to fall asleep and wondered if Dreamville wasn't real, then why did I keep seeing the woman.

"I love you, Gordon," I said as I closed my eyes.

"I love you, too, April," he said as I slipped into sleep.

Chapter Fifteen

I had no idea if I were in Dreamville or if Dreamville had become my real world. Lisa called on a daily basis to check on me and the wedding plans, none of which I remembered making.

"Good heavens, April, it's a good thing we hired a wedding planner. I do believe you've forgotten everything about the wedding. Now Rick is having his fitting this week for his tuxedo, though he is fighting me on it."

I interrupted her. "Rick's fighting you?"

"Of course," she said and paused, silent on the other end of the phone.

"He doesn't want to wear a tux and he's upset he can't take more time off for the wedding."

More silence on the other end of the phone.

"I'm sorry, Lisa. That's ridiculous. Why would Rick be recalcitrant about wearing a tux to a wedding? Did you say something to him?"

"I hardly see that you have any say in how I handle the situation with Rick," she said.

"Don't worry, Lisa. I'll talk to him."

"April, that's not necessary and if you don't understand in what an awkward situation it puts me, then you, well, hell, do what you want. I've got to go."

By now I was so agitated that I was pacing back and forth in front of the glass windows looking out onto the terrace and I was practically yelling into the phone.

I heard the click of the phone go dead on the other end and began to pound the portable phone against the back of the sofa.

"What the hell is going on?" Gordon said as he came into the room from the kitchen. "Are you fighting with Lisa again over the wedding? I don't like this extra stress, especially after you hit your head."

I shook my head.

"I'm ok. She's just being an ass about Rick and the wedding."

"Love, she just wants you to have a good wedding day. Rick can man up for one day and wear a tux. It won't kill him. Besides, if he and Lisa continue, he's going to be wearing one again soon," Gordon said, approaching me.

I stepped back from him. How did he know about the tux? Had Rick said something? Were they having conversations of which I was unaware?

He had no idea how my initial visits to Dreamville had changed our lives and he had no idea that the smallest thing might change something again. I couldn't and I wouldn't let it happen again. I didn't think I could bear it again. My poor brain was as confused as it could be.

"Can you help me on with my coat and have the car brought around? I need to drive downtown to see Rick."

"What? You're supposed to be resting this week. You do want that arm working before the wedding, don't you?"

I placed my right hand on his chest and leaned in as close as I could. If it took his desire for me to get him to see my point of view, so be it. Because he was afraid to hurt my arm, we slept together, but that was all. I knew he was on the edge sexually as I could feel his unrequited desire every night. I felt the same desire myself, but only I knew that it was truly an unfulfilled desire on my part. In his world he may have made love to me before the accident, but in my world, it had never happened. I wasn't a virgin, but I was to his lovemaking.

So, I was using it to every advantage I could. His sexual tension was a leverage I would use if it meant I could stop changes in our lives again. And so I did something I wasn't sure was either wise or advisable. I made up a story about Rick's "fragile" relationship with Lisa.

Gordon drew me closer to him and held me tightly in his arms.

"Do you really believe this?" he asked.

I looked up into his eyes, praying that he believed me.

"Yes, Gordon. I think it would hurt him. And I cannot bear the thought of that."

"Then I'll call the driver and have the car brought up. Bring Rick here and we can send the car for Lisa if you wish. Maybe have them over for dinner where we'll all be more relaxed. But, you're going to have to work through this with them. They're going to be very unhappy about it if they think you're interfering with their personal affairs."

I stood on my toes and kissed his soft lips, running my right hand along his strong jaw line.

"I love you, Gordon Stewart. You have no idea just how much."

I could feel him pull away quickly and knew why. My own body felt as tense as I'm sure his did.

"Do you want me to go with you?" he asked as I headed toward the elevator.

"No, I think he needs to talk to me first. We'll be back here before supper."

As the elevator doors closed, I could see him standing alone as he had that day at the hill when I had fallen. He looked a bit lost for a moment and instead of Gordon, the man, I saw Gordon, the 17 year old boy. And that was when I saw the woman standing behind the glass between him and the terrace. I began to push the stop button and couldn't get the elevator to stop. I ended up at the lobby before I could get the elevator car to go back to our apartment.

By the time the elevator door opened, Gordon had left the room and I panicked, not knowing where he was or if the woman had come into the room after I left. I ran to the library and through the apartment calling his name. It was only when I entered out bedroom that I saw the woman standing outside the bathroom door. What the hell had she done?

At that moment, Gordon opened the door of the bathroom and came out tightening the belt on his pants and she walked back, disappearing into the wall.

"April, what the hell is going on? I thought you had left."

"She was here, Gordon, the woman. She was standing right here. I saw her on the terrace as the elevator doors closed and I tried to get back as fast as I could, but I couldn't find you and then I saw her standing outside the door."

"April, love, this is enough. You're not going to Rick's. You need to rest. I'll call him and send the car for him. You can't go on like this. The woman is gone. She has been since we were in high school."

I sat down on the low bench at the foot of the bed. What could I say that wouldn't make him think that I had lost my mind. And now that I was in love with him, losing him was an impossible thought. How do you tell the man you love that you can't live without him and that you can't tell him what's been happening to you because you know he'll either leave you or lock you up somewhere in a posh sanitarium. I had no desire to spend the rest of my life that way and I wouldn't. God, what do I do, I thought to myself.

Then I realized he had changed the phrase about the woman from "last year" to "high school".

"I thought you said last year, not high school," I said.

"April, love, you're confused again and you really need to rest. This is far too much stress on you. I won't have you upset."

So I surrendered to him and let him call Rick. I took the Valium he gave me and laid down to sleep for awhile, knowing that I wouldn't travel to Dreamville since I was now seemed to be living there full time.

Just as the drug began to work, I thought again about his words - "The woman is gone. She has been since we were in high school." Until a few days ago, I had never seen the woman, or had I? No, I knew I had not just as certainly as I knew that Gordon had not existed in the world in which I had really resided. Did her presence have something to do with Gordon's presence in my life?

The logical part of my brain asked me why I was taking Gordon's word on everything, from the fractured elbow and the concussion as well as the woman being something my mind was dredging up from high school.

And the logical part of my brain was at war with my heart and my emotions. This man, who had never existed before a few days ago in my real life, was now my fiancé and someone with whom I was falling in love. And I had no memory of the woman before Gordon. I thought about the woman and realized that I could not describe her. Every time I thought about what her face looked like or her hair or what she was wearing, my mind's eye blurred it into just the vague shape of a woman.

I got up from the bed and felt the effects of the drug immediately. How much had he given me? I could barely stand, much less walk. Somehow I made it to the bedroom door and looked down the hall. I could hear his voice in the distance, talking to someone.

"Yes, I'm worried, but I gave her something so she would rest." He paused, then continued. "She has no idea what happened. I told her she fell skating. What the hell are you saying? I'm not telling her that. No. Absolutely not."

I heard silence then and waited for him to speak again, but he didn't. I stumbled into the living room, holding onto the door facing for support.

"Who are you?" I asked. "What did you give me? What the hell is going on?"

His face drained of color and he rushed across the room just as I was beginning to slide toward the floor. He reached his hand out to lift me up and I rolled to my right side, guarding my left arm, to try to crawl away from him.

I had been right all along. I had never known him. Was Dreamville the result of some sort of drug he was feeding me? Good god, why?

"Get away from me," I tried to say, but the words slurred together.

"April, for god's sake, what are you doing?" he asked as he lifted me and carried me back to the bedroom.

I thought I was fighting him, trying to get out of his arms, but I was just pushing against his chest. I kept saying that he didn't exist and that I was still in Dreamville, but I knew on some level that the words I was saying weren't real words. My mind was barely working.

Instead of putting me in the bed and leaving me there, he climbed onto the bed and lay down next to me, holding me against him. I could feel tears falling on my cheeks, but my body simply would not do what I wanted it to, even wiping the tears off my face.

"Don't worry, love. You're safe with me."

As I passed out from the drugs, all I could remember thinking was that I might be in more danger from him than I was from the woman I was seeing.

Chapter Sixteen

I did not awaken in what had been my real world. I woke up in the same bed where Gordon had held me down after drugging me. My head pounded as I sat up. What had he given me? I didn't care. I was getting out of there and going anywhere I could. I quietly dressed in a pair of jeans and an old Columbia sweat shirt, the entire time praying that he did not come into the room to check on me.

I found a purse in a walk-in closet the size of the bedroom from my old apartment and looked through it for anything – money, credit cards, a driver's license. Amazingly, I had picked the right purse without having to go through the others on the shelves. There wasn't much cash, but it was enough to get me to Penn Station to catch the train to Long Island. Rick and Lisa were living together there if it was still 2002 and I was still in Dreamville. They had a small apartment, but I knew I could crash on their sofa without either of them betraying my location.

I slid down the hallway, making my body as flat as I could. I couldn't hear him. I stopped at the edge of the living room and looked around the corner. I saw him outside on the terrace, talking on the phone again.

I ran to the elevator, pushed the button, and then squatted down below the center foyer table where he couldn't see me. Just as the elevator doors opened, he did see me run into the elevator, but it was too late for him. I was already gone.

By the time I reached the street, the doorman came running behind me. At first I thought he was chasing me, but I was relieved when he whistled for a passing cab to stop. He smiled at me and closed the door as I got into the cab. As I looked up to him, I was stunned to see that it was Frank, the doorman from my real world. I stared out the back window as we drove away.

The cab left me at Penn Station where I purchased a one way ticket to Hempstead. I calculated how much money I had left and found that I had barely enough to get to Rick and Lisa's. But it didn't matter. I was out of Gordon's reach. Maybe if I fell asleep at their place, I might leave Dreamville and awaken in my apartment. I leaned back into the seat and watched the passing scenery, relieved and unafraid for the first time in a week. I was going to leave Dreamville for good. I could feel it. If only my head would stop pounding, I would have felt much better.

As the cab I had hailed at the Hempstead station had dropped me off at Rick and Lisa's apartment, I wondered how I was going to explain everything to them. Thank god Rick wasn't working for Gordon yet. I knew I could depend on him. Although Rick and I had had some real fights growing up, we knew that as adults we could depend on one another completely.

I knocked on their apartment door, feeling secure in Rick's protection and almost fell down when the door opened. In the middle of their living room I saw my 'fiancé' standing there with his arms crossed against his broad chest.

Rick led me into the room and Lisa sat in a chair across the room with her head down. She had been crying and her eyes were puffy and swollen.

I jerked away from Rick and felt my elbow throb.

"What did you two do to her? Threaten her or drug her the way you did me?" I backed away from the men and moved to where Lisa was sitting. She stood, wiped her eyes, and shook her head.

"April, they haven't done anything to me. I was worried about you. You just can't go running around in your condition." She brushed my dark hair from my shoulder and hugged me. "You've got to listen, now, and not get upset. We were told you would remember, but it's only getting worse. . ."

"Lisa, stop. Enough," Rick said, interrupting her. "Gordon can take her home and take care of her. He knows what's best."

I moved behind Lisa, horrified that my brother was taking Gordon's side in this.

"No, no, no. I'm not going anywhere with him. He's been drugging me. I don't even know what the day is half the time and I don't know him. He says we've known each other since high school, but I know he's lying. He even told me it was 2002. He lies!"

Lisa turned around to face me.

"April, it is 2002. He's not lying or drugging you. You believe me, don't you?"

I sat down in the chair Lisa has previously occupied. My head hurt so much.

"It can't be 2002. It's 2011 and you two have a new baby boy and I have never seen this man until a few days ago." My head was hurting so much that I was unaware that I was holding my hands to the sides of it.

"And why was he talking to someone on the phone about giving me drugs and telling me stories about some woman I saw in his apartment? What's he hiding?"

At that point Rick sat down on the sofa. He sighed and then turned to Gordon.

"She must have heard you talking to me on the phone," he said.

I stared at my brother and could not accept what he was saying. Not Rick. No, not him.

"Rick, you don't believe me? You've always believed me. How could you do this to me? How much money is your sister worth? A job or thirty pieces of silver?"

Lisa put her hand on my right shoulder and squeezed it gently.

"April, he does care. We all care. It doesn't matter that he's working for Gordon. Gordon's been a part of your family since before I met Rick. Please trust us. Let Gordon take you home. You'll feel better tomorrow. I promise."

At that point Gordon walked across the room to me and held his hand out to me.

"You know I wouldn't hurt you for the world. Look in my eyes and tell me if you see anything but concern there. Let me take you home. The only drugs I've given you were prescribed. You can check them if you don't believe me."

I gave him my trembling hand and felt his firm grasp as he gently lifted me to my feet. He took my right elbow and steered me toward the front door. I didn't know what else to do but go with him. Rick and Lisa had been my only hope.

The drive home was silent. He sat next to me in the back of the town car and looked out the window the entire time. He made no attempt to touch me. I started to reach out to him when a sharp pain in my head made me wince. I didn't realize that I had also moaned. My head felt as if it was going to explode.

"April, are you all right?" His voice was muffled. My brain felt as if someone was playing a bass drum inside. I tried to reach up with my left arm, but it was useless. Over the drumming, I heard him tell the driver something and then he pulled a cell phone from his jacket and was talking to someone on the phone. Why couldn't I hear his words?

"We'll be there in a few minutes," seemed to be what he was saying, but the drumming in my head was louder.

The town car pulled into the emergency entrance of Columbia Presbyterian and an orderly was standing there with a wheelchair, waiting for us. Gordon ran around the car and helped me into the chair and by now I was beginning to get nauseous from the drumbeats.

"Gordon, what's wrong with me? Am I dying?" I asked, but whatever response he tried to say to me was lost in the drumbeats in my head.

The emergency staff moved me quickly into a large private room, several of them working simultaneously while Gordon had moved out of the way from the bed into a distant corner. Suddenly, the door opened and a man who looked like an older version of Gordon came into the room and started to order the people around to do specific things. His words were as muffled as everyone else's was.

I looked across the room at Gordon and held my hand out to him. He moved to my side and squeezed it tightly.

"Don't fret. My father will make sure you're fine."

The only word I heard in that sentence was 'my father' before I passed out.

It was several hours later that I came to in the same hospital bed I had been in earlier, but the room seemed different. Gordon sat in the chair next to the bed watching the traffic and the falling snow from the window. I touched his hand and he jumped.

"You're awake," he said and smiled. "You had us scared for awhile. Let me let them know you're awake now."

I watched as he opened the door and spoke to someone outside the room. He came back to the bed and took my left hand in his.

"My arm still hurts," I said. He put my hand down softly on the bed and leaned in to kiss my cheek.

"I told you it was going to take a few weeks before you could start rehab exercises, but you are the most stubborn female I've ever met. Are you sure you're not Scottish?" he said and laughed.

"What happened? My head. It hurt so much."

He pulled the hospital blanket up and smoothed my hair on the pillow.

"Don't you remember anything?"

"Well, yes, I remember everything from your phone call to arriving here, but nothing else."

It was the opportune time for his father to walk into the room.

"April, how's the head now? Anymore pain?"

"No," I said. "The headache seems to be gone now." I paused for a moment. I assumed that this was Gordon's father, but wasn't sure.

"Dr. . . . Stewart, was that a migraine? I've never had one and if it was, I never want one again."

He glanced at Gordon and then to the chart before looking at me.

"April, I know you're confused. It's only understandable after suffering a concussion, but we should let your memory return on its own. I'm afraid the episode you had was a small seizure due to the stress of your brain still trying to suppress your trauma."

"What trauma? I fell skating."

Neither man looked at me.

"Well, I did fall skating. Gordon told me I did."

His father shook his head.

"Gordon, only the truth from now on. No wonder she became confused and stressed," he said. "April, do you know how to ice skate?"

I started to say 'yes' and then realized that I had never been on an ice rink in my life.

"No, now that you ask. I remember that I don't."

I looked angrily at Gordon.

"Why the hell did you tell me I fell skating?"

He had turned a deep shade of red.

"I didn't know what to say when you woke up and didn't remember hurting your arm. I had to say something. I'm sorry. I know now that it was the wrong thing, but everyone told us that you had to remember on your own."

"Remember what? Damn it! Someone has to either tell me what's going on or I'm checking myself out of here."

Gordon's father raised his eyebrows and looked to his son.

"Would you two stop doing that? I refuse to live with secrets," I said.

I closed my eyes and held back the anger.

"I'm sorry, Dr. Stewart, that is your name, I assume, but your son, you, even my own family – what are you hiding from me?"

Gordon's father leaned the chart against the foot of the bed and looked closely at me. I could not tell if I saw concern there. I actually could not read his face at all. He might look like Gordon, but his face was nowhere near as expressive.

"April, you've known me as long as you've known Gordon and I won't lie to you. You have a right to know everything that's happened, but your neurologist believes you should allow the memories to return gradually. I can't tell you anymore than that. The answers are in your head."

I pulled my hand away from Gordon and sat up in the bed quickly, which made me feel a little punch drunk.

"And what if your answers are not the answers I find in my head? What if nothing you people tell me ever becomes real to me? What happens then?"

I could see Gordon bow his head out of the corner of my eye, but his father's gaze never left my face.

"Then you'll have to learn to live the life you have or the life you choose to make. Medically, the most we can do is to help keep you from being stressed, to tell you the truth as much as possible, and allow the damage in your brain to heal," he said.

There. The words I had dreaded. Brain. Damage. What had happened to me? How could I forget huge chunks of my life and make up almost 10 years that had never happened? I lay back down against the hospital bed and rolled away from both of them. I was suffering from brain damage he said. Dreamville existed only in my broken brain.

I closed my eyes tightly and wished to be back in the world that I had thought was real, not lying in a hospital room hearing that something was wrong with my mind. I couldn't face either of them. I just wanted to be left alone there to mourn the life I had lost or rather the life I had not lived.

"Go away. Both of you. Please now."

I didn't see Gordon look to his father for help and the dispassionate look upon his father's face, but I knew that's what was happening.

Dr. Stewart walked from the room and Gordon slowly followed him, stopping at the door to look back at me in the dimly lit room.

"Are you sure you want me to leave? I can help you if you need me," he asked.

I rolled away from him and toward the window where the snow was falling thick and fast.

"I think you've done enough. I think you should leave me here. I can stand on my own."

I heard him pause and then close the door as he left. I rolled onto my back and cradled my left elbow, which hurt but not as much as it had in the past few days.

I stared at the wall, ignoring the pain poster and the "Wash Your Hands!" poster next to it. A dry erase board was directly across from me. It had Dr. Stewart's name on it next to physician and beneath that S. Ashworth listed next to nurse.

Brain damage. This was what I had feared in what I had thought was the real world, not what I had called Dreamville. Now the world was turned upside down and I had been told that my real world had never existed.

I wondered if I had a business or where I had been since the last time I remembered seeing Gordon. I also wondered why Lisa had chattered on about a wedding as if everything was perfectly normal. How could she? May parents. How could they not call?

I realized I had not spoken to anyone other than Rick, Lisa and Gordon or his father in the last few days. If this was the real world, where were my parents, David, or Carl, even my grandmother? And why hadn't Gordon or my brother called my folks to let them know I was in the hospital.

I looked at the phone on the bed table. I had no idea what time it was, but I was going to call my mom and dad. Someone was going to answer my questions. Someone had to.

I punched in my family's number and waited for an answer. I was stunned when I heard a computer voice inform me that the number had been temporarily disconnected. Disconnected? My folks had had that number for decades. They wouldn't have moved and Carl was still living with them as well as my grandmother. The commute was easier for him and he did not want to live in Manhattan. He attended Yale and it just made more sense to stay at home.

I dialed Rick's number. Damn it, he was going to tell me why my folks' number was disconnected. I didn't care what time it was. He should be here anyway. Why hadn't anyone from my family come here? Damn Gordon. He probably hadn't bothered to call any of them.

Rick answered the phone on the eighth ring. He sounded as if he had been asleep for hours.

"Rick, I'm in the hospital. Something happened when Gordon drove me back to the city," I said.

Before I could continue, he said, "I know, April. You're getting released in the morning. Gordon said you were okay. Do you know it's 3 a.m.?"

"Rick, you know I don't care what Gordon told you. You should have come or at least have called mom or dad. I tried to call them and the number's been disconnected."

I could hear dead silence on the other end and then muffled voices as if he were discussing something with Lisa while his hand was covering the phone.

"Get some rest, April. We'll see you at your place tomorrow. OK?"

I became furious.

"And where the hell is my place, Rick? Why aren't Mom and Dad here? I don't care what time it is. What's going on?"

"April, I'm hanging up and going back to sleep. We'll talk tomorrow at your and Gordon's apartment. Good night," he said and hung up.

I held the beige receiver in my hand and stared at it. He hung up on me! I weighed my options at that moment. I was so angry that I almost started to get up to dress and leave, but if I had had some sort of seizure, I knew that was a bad idea.

I placed the receiver back on the phone cradle and crawled deep into the bed after turning off the light above the bed. Outside I could see the snowflakes glittering in the streetlight. I dozed off, wishing I could leave this Dreamville and go back to my "real world."

Chapter Seventeen

And my real world was exactly where I was when I awoke. I was in the guest room at Gordon's empty apartment once more. I jumped from the bed to look out the window to see dry streets without snow. Where was I? Was this Dreamville or was it the life I had thought I had lived all along?

I cleaned up and dressed and went into the sparsely furnished apartment. No Edward Hopper painting in the foyer. Only that ugly hospital green sofa and the few chairs that had been there yesterday.

Yesterday. When was yesterday? Yesterday I had been in a hospital bed in 2002 with some sort of brain damage that had "robbed" me of certain memories and created false ones. Yet, here I was, standing in the middle of Gordon's huge and empty apartment. How much more "real" could this be?

I pinched my arm and it hurt. If this was Dreamville, did pinches hurt? And then there was the question of the swimsuit and the sunburn. I wasn't sunburned and my arm felt fine. Was I dreaming the sunburn? Was I dreaming the broken elbow?

I sat down on the couch for a moment and pondered the possibilities of my situation. Either I had been having very vivid dreams in the place I had dubbed Dreamville or this was a hallucination caused by brain damage in what I had been told was the real world.

I heard Gordon in the kitchen and made my decision quickly without a second thought. I left the apartment and jumped in a taxi to take me to Soho to my apartment building where I found Frank, my doorman, on duty. I wasn't sure if I was relieved to see him there. The last time I had tried to run from Gordon, Frank had been the doorman at Gordon's building.

"Ms. Norris. Good to see you back. Are you going to be here for a while?"

I leaned against the counter and spoke in a conspiratorial whisper.

"Frank, if anyone, and I mean anyone, comes here looking for me or calls for me, tell them I'm not here. I want to avoid some people, if you know what I mean."

He frowned. Frank did not like lying to anyone. One reason I liked him so much.

"Are you sure that's what you want? I mean, after what happened the other day, are you sure you want to do that?"

"Absolutely," I said and smiled broadly. I wanted to stay in this world and it seemed that every time I came in contact with Gordon Stewart, my life was turned upside down. I felt briefly that even seeing the strange woman was less dangerous than seeing Stewart.

I opened my apartment and remembered that Stewart had had Lisa remove some of my clothes and toiletries. Well, they can be replaced. Mr. Gordon Stewart was going to be out of my life for good.

I went to the kitchen and found the milk and eggs were still fresh. I grabbed them and made myself a plate of scrambled eggs and orange juice. Unfortunately, the bread was bad so toast wasn't on the menu. But I ate the eggs as if I hadn't tasted food this good in ages.

I was rinsing the dishes and putting them in the empty dishwasher when the phone began to ring. I ignored it and unplugged it from the wall. Then my iPhone began ringing. I turned it off and went into my living room and turned the television on. The women on The View were discussing the upcoming presidential race. Oh god, it felt so good to be back in a world where I felt I belonged, a world I knew had to be real.

I finally gathered the courage to go back to my bedroom and bathroom. At first I was afraid that the strange woman would be there, but she was gone. The place felt safe and I threw myself on the bed and felt relaxed.

I should have known that neither Gordon nor Rick would have left me alone. I had two hours of peace and quiet before I heard the pounding on the door. Just as I was deciding not to answer it, thinking it was Gordon and Rick, I heard the voice of an unknown man saying, "NYPD, ma'am. Please open the door."

Damn, I thought. I had almost made a clean get away. I had forgotten briefly about the police being called the last time I was here. I went to the door, saw the officer through the peephole, and unchained the door to open it.

"Ms. Norris? Is everything okay here?" he asked, but before he could finish, my brother pushed past him and came into my apartment.

"April, what the hell? Gordon and I have been looking everywhere for you!"

I looked to the officer and offered him an apologetic smile.

"Yes, officer. I'm fine. I'm sorry you were called out for nothing. Thank you for your concern," I said and was shutting the door behind him just as Gordon came past him and into the room.

I sighed. There was no getting away from this man. I looked at him and thought that he looked a little more handsome as an older man than he had at 25. He seemed more sure of himself, more experienced. And unfortunately, much more attractive to me.

"Rick, I'm fine. No one here but me. I'm not leaving my place. I have a business to run and I like my life just as it is."

Although I was speaking to Rick, I was aiming my words right at Stewart. Neither man was listening to me.

"And what about this woman who's stalking you?" Rick asked. "What if she shows up again and you're here alone? Do you think Mom and Dad could go through losing you after David? How selfish are you?"

I sat down at the island in the kitchen and drummed my fingers against the countertop. It suddenly reminded me of the drumbeats in my head that landed me in the hospital in Dreamville. I stopped my fingers immediately and looked at both of them.

"Rick, don't be ridiculous. I am not going anywhere and I want my life back. Go home to your family. I'll be okay."

Gordon stood across the room with his arms at his waist. He shook his head and turned to the door.

"Ms. Norris, I'm glad you're fine though it would have been considerate of you to have let someone know where you were. Rick, I'll see you at the office tomorrow. We can start interviews for staff," he said and left.

Rick watched Gordon leave and then headed toward the door himself.

"April, I don't know what the hell is wrong with you, but your stupid antics could cost me this job. Please don't screw it up for me."

And then he was gone as well.

I went to the door and locked and chained it again. I decided to leave the phones off and went back into the living room and spent the afternoon watching bad talk shows and a soap opera called The Bold and the Beautiful, which made me giggle. They should have my problems, I thought and switched the channel to watch an old movie on TCM.

The afternoon passed so pleasantly that I briefly forgot about Dreamville, or Gordon Stewart or the woman, And that, of course, was the worst mistake of the week.

At first, I thought it was just a flash of light at the corner of my eye, but then I saw a quick movement and turned to look around the room. Nothing. I went back to the movie and had almost forgotten seeing the flash of light when I looked up to see the woman standing next to the sofa. I flew across the room to the kitchen door and watched her walk toward me.

I ran to the bathroom and locked the door. I could hear her breathing outside the bathroom door.

"Go away!" I yelled. "Leave me alone!"

Just as I thought she had left I watched as she walked through the solid door. I stumbled backwards and tripped on the towels I had left there yesterday. As my feet flew out from under me, I knew two things – I was going to land on my left elbow and that I was going to hit my head on the tiled floor and that I would hit it hard enough to knock me out.

Just before the lights went out in my head, I heard the woman speak for the first time.

"Bitch, shut up or you'll be dead, too."

Chapter Eighteen

When I woke up this time and saw the snow on the window ledge in the morning light, I almost cried. What did I have to do to stay in one place? I wanted to go back home to a time when no one wanted to hurt me and I had a normal life. Both Dreamville and the real world were both becoming too frightening. I remembered the woman's words. I shivered under the thin blanket as a tall thin nurse entered the room and smiled at me. Nurse Ashworth, I guessed, since her name was still on the board and on the badge on her coat.

"Head feeling better this morning?" she asked as she put a blood pressure cuff around my arm and placed a pulse meter on my finger. She watched the computer screen and then just as quickly removed everything.

"Can I leave?" I asked her.

She shrugged slightly as she used a computer tablet to input my vitals. She seemed friendly enough, but she also seemed to be busy. Her movements were efficient and smooth.

"Depends on your doctor, though I do think I saw your name on the discharge list. Once Dr. Stewart sends up any discharge orders, you should be able to get out of here."

I tried to sit up on the side of the bed and other than feeling as if I had a mild hangover, I didn't feel too bad considering I was sitting in a hospital room. I saw a small closet next to the bathroom and decided that my clothes would probably be there, but I was wrong. Nothing. Damn. Gordon had either taken my clothes or they had been lost somewhere between the ER and the room.

As I was walking back to the bed, I heard a soft knock on the door and Rick and Lisa walked in. Lisa ran to me and hugged me.

"You look good, all things considered," she said and grinned.

I smiled at her, but ignored my brother. He, I didn't have to be friendly to after last night.

"C'mon, April. What could he have done at three in the morning? Don't be mad. Between the weather and Gordon being with you, we knew you would be okay without us rushing over here," she said.

They hadn't quite closed the door when they entered the room and I could hear Gordon's voice outside the door. He was arguing with his father over me, but I couldn't quite hear everything.

Rick saw me gazing out the door and swiftly went to it and closed it.

I shook my head and sighed loudly.

"What is it with you? You never used to be such a jerk!"

His face paled and I could see that I had truly hurt him with my words. Well, good, I thought. Hang up on me. You get what you deserve.

Instead of speaking to me, he spoke to his wife.

"I told you coming here was a bad idea. We should have just let Gordon take her home."

I was so shocked by his words that my jaw literally dropped. Now I was really angry with him.

"Well, then just go! Obviously, you have no need for your sister anymore than your family. Did you even call the family? I suppose it's just easier to let Gordon take care of your brain damaged and crazy sister."

He snorted and then started to say something, but Lisa jumped up and stood between him and my bed. He bent his head, rubbed his eyes and looked outside as if he hadn't a clue what to say to me. And worst of all, he looked sad. Were things that bad for me? I hadn't seen that look on his face since the real summer Lucy had dumped him in high school.

Lisa stroked his arm and touched his face as if to calm him. He turned from her and left the room. She stood there for a few seconds before turning back to face me. It was as if she were putting on a different face to use with me and for the first time I saw a falseness there. She was trying to be kind for Rick, not me, and I thought I could see a glimmer of anger in her eyes that did not match the smile her mouth was forming.

"He's been so worried and tied up with work. Give him a break, April. He's doing his best, too. I mean, you're not the only one who's been affected by this, this situation."

I was puzzled by the word she used - situation. How the hell could I know what the situation was if no one would tell me what was going on?

Just as I started to ask her about the "situation", Dr. Stewart came breezing into the room, followed by Gordon and Rick. Dr. Stewart had the same dispassionate look he had worn last night, but Gordon had a mix of anger and something else on his face. Rick still looked sad.

"April, you're free to go. You need to take it easy and you'll need to see Dr. Fritcher next week. Your memory could just come back and it might not come back at all."

"Everyone here is following Dr. Fritcher's instructions, so don't blame them for not answering all your questions. Your MRI looks good, so once your elbow's healed, physically you should be able to get back to a normal life."

Normal life? I almost laughed at that. My life hadn't been normal for over a week now, maybe longer. Wonder how normal he would think I was if I started telling him that this was Dreamville and that another world was real to me?

"Do you have any questions," he said, more than asked.

"No, wait, should you be treating someone who's about to be in your family?" I just had to push one more button.

He laughed and walked away, patting Gordon's shoulder as he left.

I rolled my eyes at his failure to respond and raised my good arm and slapped the bed with my hand.

"Did anyone think to bring me clothing or am I going to be discharged in this oh so stylish and backless hospital gown?" I asked sarcastically.

Gordon came over to the bed table and opened the lower compartment and lifted my clothes onto the bed. Well, Nancy Drew, I wasn't. That was for sure. I hadn't even thought to look there.

"Could I have some privacy?"

Rick and Lisa went to the door, but Gordon remained.

"That means you, too, Stewart."

He didn't budge, but folded his arms across his chest in the same way I had seen him do in my kitchen. Wow. I could see the man he was instead of the kid from high school and I shut my mouth and dressed with my back to him.

As I was trying to pull on my leather boots, my elbow was refusing to cooperate. He came to my side of the bed and knelt there to pull each boot on my feet. I blushed at his kindness after I had been such a bitch to him. If only I could figure out what was going on, I might really come to care about him. No matter what stunt I had pulled or what I had said, he had maintained an equanimity in the face of all of it.

"Thanks," I said, almost in a whisper.

"What did you say?" he asked, looking up at me.

"I said 'Thanks'," I replied.

"I'm sorry," he said, "I couldn't quite make that out, could you say it a little louder?"

He was grinning and I realized that he had heard me from the beginning.

"I said 'Thanks'," yelling as loudly as I could.

He stood, lifted me to my feet and hugged me tight against his body. He kissed me lightly on the my cheek.

"You're very welcome," he said just as an orderly rolled a wheelchair into the room and Nurse Ashworth followed with a sheaf of papers for me to sign. I half listened to her instructions as I signed my name to what seemed like countless papers. She handed half of them back to me and wished me good luck as she quickly left the room.

The orderly waited with a smile, leaning against the handles at the back of the chair. He was a tall man and wide, with bright red hair. While he couldn't have been much older than I was, he was intimidating, smile and all.

"I really don't need a wheelchair," I said.

The orderly grinned and his deep voice matched his size.

"Dr. Stewart's orders and I think you know we're not going to argue with his orders."

I was surprised to see Rick and Lisa still waiting in the hall as the orderly rolled me out of the room with Gordon following. Rick looked to Gordon and I glanced up to see a smile on Gordon's face. Rick's face seem to relax all at once and it seemed as if all the tension went out of his body at the same time.

"Come over to our flat," Gordon said to them. "I'm having lunch picked up at the deli down the street and we can eat and make her watch."

I half turned in the chair only to realize that Gordon was teasing me about not getting to eat. I faced forward again and took a deep breath as we went to the bank of elevators.

And that was when I really saw the woman for the first time. Clearly saw her. She couldn't have been more than 25, with dirty blonde hair, jeans and a ratty looking black ski jacket. This time I could see her face and something in my head seemed to click into place. I had seen her before. I couldn't remember where, but she was real, whether I was in Dreamville or not. This woman was real in both worlds.

"It's her!" I yelled and pointed at the woman. "That's the woman I keep seeing!"

I expected all of them to ignore my outburst and so I was stunned when Rick and Gordon ran down the hall towards the woman, who had heard my outburst. She took off down the hall and disappeared behind the stairwell door before the men got to her.

Lisa had grabbed my right hand and her face had drained of all color.

The elevators arrived, but the orderly didn't move.

"Lisa, she's real. I'm not imagining her. She's real."

"Yes, April, she's very real," Lisa almost whispered. She turned to the orderly and told him to take me back to the nurse's station and pulled out a card and told him to call it immediately.

"Lisa, who is she? Has she been stalking me here, too?"

Lisa was too engrossed in getting me back to the nurses' station and watching for Rick and Gordon to answer my question or notice that I had used the word 'here'. After about 10 minutes, Rick and Gordon came back up on the elevator.

"We lost her," Rick said despondently. "She disappeared somewhere on one of the floors between here and the garage. Did anyone call the police?"

Gordon's face was an angry red.

"Damn, how could she have gotten away so fast? We were right behind her," he said, still a bit out of breath from the pursuit.

"Will someone tell me what the hell is going on? Who is she and why do I keep seeing her everywhere?" I demanded from them.

"Tell me. I thought I was going crazy, that she was a product of my damaged brain, but that was a real person. I saw her clearly. You guys did, too. Who is she?"

Gordon leaned down to me in the chair.

"Love, I'm going to have to ask you to go back into the hospital room while we talk to the police. You're going to have to trust me on this. But the fact that you remembered her is good. It's very good."

"No, no, Gordon, don't," I said, but the orderly already was moving me back into the room.

I was so frustrated. For the first time I could remember the woman's face, the face I was seeing here and in my real world. Why couldn't I hear what they were talking to the police about? Why couldn't I talk to the police? If I were the one she was stalking, then I had the right to talk to them.

I decided to ignore the three of them and stood from the wheelchair and started toward the door, only to be blocked by the orderly. I had thought he was large before, but standing in front of him, I saw that he was the size of a linebacker. There was no way I could get past him.

"I'm sorry, ma'am. You're going to have to stay here. Mr. Stewart is right. They can take of this and then you can go home. Don't you want that?" he spoke to me as if I were a child, which irritated me as much as his blocking my way with his body.

"You don't understand . . ."

He shook his head. There was no way I was going to get past him unless . . .

I suddenly put my hand to my head pretended to be in pain. He led me to the bed and went out the door, presumably to get Nurse Ashworth. He had no idea that I was on his heels as he exited the room. Just as I saw Gordon and Rick talking to a man and woman, the orderly saw my deception and tried to restrain me. I feinted left as he reached for my right arm and I managed to escape him and put myself in front of the police officers.

"Ms. Norris, should you be here?" the woman asked.

I recognized Detective Sanchez and Detective Dan from my real world. What were they doing in Dreamville? Perhaps the woman here was the woman stalking me in my real life. But before I could respond, Gordon took my left arm above the elbow and led me back to the large orderly.

"Oww, Gordon, let go. You're hurting my arm."

"I am not. I am not near your elbow. Now stop playing games and do as I asked."

I used my right arm to try to push him away. Did he really tell me to do as he asked? I became very angry, but his grip on my arm was too tight and the orderly took me by the shoulders and directed me back into the hospital room. The entire time I was cursing both of them and calling the detectives to assist me, but they ignored my pleas as well.

I was calling the orderly and Gordon every foul name I could think of and the orderly was actually grinning with every new insult I threw at him.

"You have quite a potty mouth for such a proper little thing," he said. "The only time I've heard language like that was from a little meth addict, but she was a lot stronger than you."

I shut my mouth and walked back to the chair next to the bed and looked out the window. They could not keep me here. I had been discharged from the hospital and legally they had no right to restrain me. I suddenly remembered that my Dad would be at his law office. I calmly walked over to the phone and began to dial his number. The orderly ignored me as his only task was to keep me in the room. No one had told him to stop me from using the telephone.

"Brooks, Steiner and Norris," the receptionist answered.

I smiled broadly. Reinforcements were imminent.

"Yes, I'd like to speak with Adam Norris please," I said. Across the room, the orderly was starting to think about what I was doing. I turned my back to him and lowered my voice to avoid raising any doubts in his mind about what I was doing.

"I'm sorry, Mr. Norris is not here," she said.

"Listen, this is his daughter, April. I have to speak to him immediately. Is he in a meeting or in court? It's urgent that I speak with him as soon as possible."

Silence on the other end of the phone, then she responded, "Ms. Norris, could you hold, please?"

"Of course," I said and felt a small smile tugging at the corners of my mouth. Keep me a prisoner! My brother and Mr. Stewart were going to pay for this. My father would be very angry by the situation.

As I waited, I remembered Lisa's use of the word 'situation' and something was tugging at the back of my mind. I couldn't name it, but something wasn't right, which was proved when Richard Brooks answered the phone instead of my father.

"April, how lovely to hear from you. I assume you're feeling better now. Your arm must be healing well. What can I do for you?"

"You can put my father on the phone. I'm at the hospital, from which I was just discharged, but no one will allow me to leave, including two police detectives outside. They have a large orderly blocking my way. I need my father to come down here and put a stop to this."

Again, silence on the other end. I was beginning to think that the only way out of this mess was to get in the bed and try to go to sleep. Maybe then I'd wake up in the real world.

"April, um, what's the name of the hospital and what floor is your room? I'll take care of this for your dad, don't worry."

I sighed. Dad must be in court or I wouldn't be stuck with Richard.

"I'm at Columbia Presbyterian on the third floor. Could you hurry? I really want to talk to Dad and there's nothing wrong with me physically. Dr. Stewart told me that when he discharged me."

"Not a problem. I'll be on it as soon as we hang up. Okay?"

"Thanks, Mr. Brooks. I don't even think Rick told my parents that I was here last night. I really appreciate your help with this."

We said good-bye to one another and I sat back down in the chair and looked smugly at the orderly. Surprisingly, he did not look angry, but he did have an odd look on his face that I couldn't quite decipher. He walked out the door and closed it firmly behind him. I could hear him talking to Rick and Gordon.

I expected him to come back into the room, but instead Gordon came in.

"Ready to go?" he asked as if nothing had happened.

I refused to look at him.

"I called my father. He's on his way. You and Rick did one thing wrong – you kept me here against my will and refused to allow me to talk to the police. I won't be leaving with you. I'm going to my folks. I've had it with you and my brother."

I continued to ignore him. The silence in the room was almost unbearable, but I felt I had made my point. Round one, me.

"Did you actually talk to your Dad?"

I turned to him. Who the hell did he think he was?

"Well, no, I talked with his partner, Richard Brooks, but Brooks is taking care of the situation. He's making sure my folks are aware of what you and Rick have done."

Gordon walked around the bed and sat on the edge of it next to the chair where I sat. He looked down at his hands and then out the window at the white world the snow had left Manhattan enveloped within.

"April, um, Brooks called the nurses' station. He talked with the detectives and then with me. He requested that I take you back to our apartment, especially since we saw the woman here at the hospital."

My mouth gaped open at his revelation. Damn Richard Brooks!

"But my folks. Is that what they want me to do?"

Gordon sighed and then brushed a dark strand of hair from my cheek and smiled.

"Yes, April. It's where you live now. It's where you belong."

I stood and looked up at him. I didn't know whether to punch him and run away again or just follow him. Instead, I walked to the door.

"Don't you want your carriage?"

I looked at the wheelchair with disdain.

"You know as well as I do that I do not need that nor am I going to ride in it again," I said and walked into the hallway.

This time Rick and Lisa were gone and only Nurse Ashworth and the orderly were at the nurses' station. She smiled and said good-bye, but the orderly could not look at me. It was if he were hiding from me.

I didn't care. I was leaving this place and heaven forbid that I ever see it again. By the time Gordon and I had made it to his building, I was resigned to whatever fate Dreamville was holding for me. I believed that once I was asleep that I would return to the real world and now that I knew whom the woman was, I could fight back. She wasn't a ghost or a ghoul or any sort of nightmare. She was a real person who seemed intent on making me miserable. I believed that if I could stop her, then I could stop these awful trips to Dreamville every time I fell asleep. It would be so wonderful to go home again and stay there.

Then I thought of going to my folks. If I didn't wake from Dreamville tomorrow, I could take the train up to Connecticut to see them and get away from this whole nightmare for a few days. Either way, it would be good to see everyone.

I felt Gordon's stare and faced him. He looked away as the car pulled up to the building.

Frank, the doorman in both worlds, was waiting for the car and quickly came to open the door for me.

Gordon exited the car without his help and came round to where I stood to lead me into the building. I quickly pulled away from him.

"I neither need nor desire your assistance," I said to him and marched to the elevator where I jabbed at the up button. I could feel his presence behind me, but I refused to respond to him. I looked toward the desk where Frank had gone to sit and thought that it looked oddly like the one in my own apartment building in Soho.

As the elevator doors opened, I walked away and over to where Frank sat. Gordon had moved to the elevator doors and stood there holding them open, waiting for me.

"Frank, how long have your worked here?"

He looked up in surprise.

"Well, Ms. Norris, I've been here about 10 years, before you and Mr. Stewart moved in last month."

"Last month?" I asked.

"Yes, ma'am. Remember when we . . ."

Suddenly the elevator emergency bell sounded, cutting off Frank's response.

Gordon came over to me and took me by the arm.

"We have people waiting upstairs, April. You can talk to Frank later. Come now," he said, pulling me away as he had in the hospital.

Once we were in the elevators with the doors closed, I began to curse him and every Scottish ancestor he had ever had.

"How dare you keep pushing me around? I'm not your property. I'm not even your wife and if I were, you certainly wouldn't be doing this. I can't believe my family is allowing this to continue."

He said nothing and did not look at me.

"Fine, then. The wedding is off," I said. "Oh, and for the record, if the concussion did damage my memory, I should tell you that I do not remember ever having been with you, not kissing you or making love to you or even agreeing to marry you!"

He roughly pulled me over to his body and kissed me hard, his mouth exploring mine with such pressure that I was breathless when he pushed me back from him.

"Now you have something to remember," he said and the elevator doors opened. He briskly walked away from me and left me standing in the elevator as he threw his leather gloves on the foyer table and went into the apartment.

I walked slowly out of the elevator and stood at the table and looked down at it. There was one thing that I was sure of at that moment, just as I had been sure of seeing the woman at the hospital – Gordon Stewart had never really kissed me before that moment and I was positive we had never made love.

My hands were trembling as I walked to the guest room. My life was not right and somehow I knew it never would be again, Dreamville or no Dreamville.

Chapter Nineteen

After three more weeks in Dreamville, I began to despair that I would ever make it back to my real world. Outside, the world stayed cold, grey and blustery. Inside, the atmosphere was not much different. I rarely saw Gordon and the few times I ventured outside, the raw winds that blew through the streets of Manhattan cut into me, leaving my cheeks wind burned and raw.

Gordon seldom spoke to me after the incident in the elevator. I had gone into the guest room that day and had left Gordon, Rick and Lisa alone and they had left me alone as well. I supposed that Gordon had told them that I wanted to cancel the wedding, but they never spoke of it. Actually, after that day, I hadn't spoken to them at all.

I tried to call my parents, but could not reach them. My father's receptionist informed me that they were in London where my father was working on a complicated case. When I pressed her for more information, I received what seemed to be the party line every time I called – they were traveling quite a bit, but she would try to get a message to them.

I took the train up to Connecticut the next day as I had planned, but I found the house locked up and the spare keys gone. I searched my purse for keys, but found none, not even to Gordon's. At the house, the drapes were drawn tight and I couldn't see anything inside. I wondered where my grandmother and Carl were. They, at least, should have been there.

Neither David nor Rick would return my calls and so I was forced to return to Gordon's apartment. He was waiting in the living room reading when I returned. As much as I did not want to do so, I was forced to ask him if he knew where my family was.

He shrugged and left the room. He was still angry, I supposed, and I guessed that I should start looking for somewhere else to live. The problem was that I had no real money, no business or job that I knew of, and because I had always been rather solitary, no real friends other than my family. I was stuck in Dreamville in a very comfortable prison. Every night I prayed that I would wake up in my real world and every morning I found myself alone in Gordon's guest room.

One day I took a cab to Soho to where my shop would have been. Even at 25, I was already in business there so logically the shop should be there. But I was discovering that there was nothing logical about Dreamville. Instead of my shop, where at the time I still would have been sleeping in the back, I found a clothing boutique that seemed to be thriving.

I entered the store and walked around. It looked fresh and the clothing was not cheap. I spoke with one of the shop girls and pretended to be new to the neighborhood. I asked her how long they had been there.

"Oh, I think Kate opened the shop about three years ago. She got a great deal on the lease and I think she's done well here."

I smiled and thanked her then left and walked in the direction of where my apartment building would be. Three years would have been about the time I had found the empty storefront and began my own adventures in antiques, repurposing and decorating. What had I been doing the last three years in Dreamville? Where had I lived before I had moved into Gordon's place? Of course, since none of this was real, I decided that the empty spaces in my memory were normal. My mind simply hadn't made up a story to fill in that time.

But, somehow I knew that wasn't right. It didn't feel right. My 'real' world seemed to be slipping further and further from me. Nothing would make that clearer than when I realized that I had walked past where my apartment building should have been. The address from my real world was a bar and restaurant in Dreamville. I stood outside the windows of the bar and watched the crowded tables filled with people laughing, drinking, and talking.

The street was empty except for me standing in front of the spot where my apartment building should have been. I had never felt lonelier in my life than I did at that moment. I walked back down the street till I saw a cab and had the driver take me back to Gordon's.

Frank was there, quick to open the cab door for me and welcome me home. I gave him a small, sad smile and felt myself giving up. I had never been so lost in my life and the only place I had to go was a place I did not recognize nor feel welcome. Depression overwhelmed me. I believed it was because of being stuck in Dreamville, but inside I knew it was something more than that. I wondered if it was how I had left things with Gordon. All I knew was that nothing felt right.

The only reason I had any money at all was that I knew that Gordon was putting money in my wallet. Not that I was spending much other than cab fare and for the train trip to Connecticut, but every morning I found the wallet refreshed with more money than I would really need.

I found myself spending more and more time standing on the terrace, staring out at the mostly empty park, mourning the life that had seemed to slip away from me. One day when I was standing out there, tears began to slide down my cheek and the warmth of them left trails across my wind burned cheeks.

I had turned my face away from the wind and saw Gordon standing on the other side of the glass with a look of pity on his face. I couldn't bear his pity and looked away for a brief moment, but when I turned back to look at him, silently hoping that he would reach out for me, call me in out of the weather and hold me, he was gone. I sat down on a stone bench and wept so hard that my whole body shook.

Several hours after that, he knocked at the guest room door. I wanted to apologize and I wanted him to apologize and I knew that we were both too stubborn to do either.

"April," he said from the other side of the door, "I wanted to remind you that you have an appointment with Dr. Fritcher tomorrow morning at 10 o'clock"

I jumped up from the bed and ran to open the door, but he was already gone. I felt like I was living with a stranger, which was really true. Outside of a few times in my real world, I had never seen Gordon anywhere other than in Dreamville.

I walked down the hall to his library, but it was empty. I went to the foyer, but didn't see him in the living room or hear him in the kitchen. Without thinking I walked to where "our" bedroom had been and opened the door. He was in the middle of preparing to shower and had nothing on but a towel wrapped around his tightly muscled waist. I knew immediately that I should have turned away and left, but I could not take my eyes off him. I suddenly laughed, more out of nerves than anything else, thinking that

Dreamville had at least given me something interesting to look at.

"Is there something you want?" he asked coldly, ignoring both my smile and small laugh.

I sobered up at once and apologized and ran to the hall closet to grab my coat and purse, and for once did not have to wait for the elevator. I was so embarrassed. How stupid of me to have just entered his room.

Before the elevator doors could close, he slipped through them, still wearing only the towel. My eyes were moist with tears and wide with shock that he had followed me.

"April, come back home. I'm sorry I was rude. You surprised me. After you said the wedding was off, I was angry and I had no idea what to say to you. Please come back."

Just as he finished speaking the elevator stopped on one of the lower floors and an older woman swathed in what I presumed to be mink started to enter the car, but when seeing Gordon's state of undress, she jumped back from the elevator into the hallway. As the doors closed, I looked at Gordon and we both burst out laughing. He hit the stop button, and then restarted the elevator up to his place.

He pulled the towel up a bit and tried to close it completely, but it would not meet and left part of his left thigh bare.

He looked up at the numbers and his face had turned red this time.

"I suppose I should have thought about what I had on before I jumped into the elevator," he said.

I placed my hand over my mouth to suppress the laughter that was threatening to spill out.

"Go ahead. Laugh," he said, and then turned to smile at me. "But at least you're coming back home. If I knew going out in February in a towel would have helped the situation, I would have done it weeks ago."

I became pensive as we walked back into his apartment. There was that word 'situation' again. But before my mind went down that path, he had put his hand on my shoulder to relax me as if I were an easily startled mare. I moved closer to him and put my own hand on his chest, tracing a line down his chest with my finger. How could he seem so familiar and yet his body seem like unknown territory to me?

Taking my touch as an invitation he pulled me to him and kissed me the way he had the last time we had touched on the elevator. I responded, feeling such need of him, and I felt him pulling my coat away and lifting me up onto the antique marble and mahogany table in the foyer.

He tugged my skirt up and pulled the towel away from his body as I wrapped my legs around his waist and returned his kisses with a desperation I had not felt in months.

As he entered me, I slid further back onto the table and he climbed on top of me as our bodies began to move quickly and hard against one another, straining together, lost in the moment of discovering each other.

When we came together and our entwined bodies were still locked in place, I suddenly realized that we had broken the large Limoges vase that had sat in the center of the table.

"I think should get off the table before we break it as well as the vase."

"Forget the vase," he said and carried me back to our bedroom. "We can take care of those things later."

And for the first time, I didn't want to leave Dreamville. After we made love again, I tried to stay awake, afraid that when I woke that he might not be there holding me. God, I thought, please let me stay here, as I realized that I would be lost forever without him in my life. I was torn at that moment, wanting to never be without him and yet wanting to know what was wrong with me.

He fell asleep long before I did, his arms wrapped around me, one leg thrown over both of mine. I rolled onto my right side and fit my body next to his. I realized that no matter what was going on that I had fallen in love with him. If I stayed in Dreamville, my real life, ten years, would be gone. If I finally escaped to my real life, I would not know him the way I knew him now. He would be Rick's employer and a customer I was helping to decorate his apartment. He would not know about this night we had spent together and he might never feel anything about me other than just a casual acquaintance.

And that's where my real quandary came to bear. Give up my life or risk losing him. And then, I thought, there was always the chance that none of this was real, that I was in a coma or something worse, or that I would spend the rest of my life moving back and forth between Dreamville and the real world, which was becoming more of a dream than Dreamville was.

I tried to sleep, but I could not stop the fears from invading my thoughts. By the time the dim sun was coming through the drapes, I was so confused and distraught that I thought that I might not be able to survive this nightmare my life had become.

I knew when he woke up when he began to kiss my bare shoulder. I rolled onto my back and looked into his eyes and knew that the chances were not in my favor for staying with him since the real world had had a longer hold on me. I buried my face against his shoulder. Why had this happened to me? It was all so unfair.

"Does your elbow hurt from last night?" he asked stroking my arm.

I shook my head and lifted my tear stained face to kiss him before he could see that I had been crying. We made love slowly that morning, savoring each second we had together – he, because I had been absent from his life and his bed, me because I had never felt his touch before, had never felt love for him before now.

I wanted to tell him everything that morning and looking back, perhaps I should have. Later events would not have been so difficult. But hindsight is always 20/20, even when you think you know what will happen anyway.

Gordon had his car drive us to Dr. Fritcher's office, though I had no idea whom he was. I told Gordon that he didn't have to go with me, that I promised to come back, but he refused, saying that he wanted to be there for me.

As we approached Fritcher's office, I was surprised to see a small plaque next to his office door with just his name and beneath it the word "psychiatrist". I was seeing a shrink? Why? The concussion and the mysterious accident that had caused it?

"Gordon, have we been here before?" I asked as we walked into an empty waiting room.

"Yes, love, several times since the accident. Do you not remember?" He looked frightened as if my brain was losing more memories and I began to fear the way he looked at me.

"Why don't I remember?"

He shrugged and as we sat down, took my hand in his and twined our fingers together.

"It doesn't matter. As long as we're together, things will be okay."

I tried to smile, but trepidation filled my head and my gut was doing flip-flops. The door into Fritcher's office opened and a friendly looking man in his mid 50s opened the door and smiled broadly at me.

"April, how are you today? Come in and let's get started so we can have a nice chat. I made some of the orange pekoe tea you like," Fritcher said and held the door open for me.

I left my coat and purse with Gordon and looked back at him once more as I walked through the door, afraid that I would never see him again if I went into that room. He smiled and waved at me as if to reassure me, but I still hesitated slightly before I closed the door behind me.

In Fritcher's office, the sweet smell of orange tea filled the air. I hated orange pekoe tea, but I somehow couldn't remember ever drinking it, either. I couldn't imagine why he would have fixed it for me. Was it normal for shrinks to offer tea to their patients? I had no idea. As far as I was concerned, I had never met one before this day.

I sat down in an armchair across from where Dr. Fritcher had already sat down and waited as he poured the tea.

"You seem to be having less trouble with your elbow," he said as he handed me a small china teacup and saucer.

"Yes, it's feeling quite a bit better."

I sniffed at the tea. I hated the smell of it, but it reminded me of something. What was it that I couldn't remember?

I sat the cup and saucer down on the table next to the chair.

"I'm sorry, Dr. Fritcher, but have I told you that I liked tea? And I might as well tell your this – I don't remember ever meeting you before this morning."

He chuckled and then sipped at his tea.

"Orange Pekoe isn't my favorite, either, but I was hoping the smell and taste of it might help you remember."

"Remember what?"

He took a deep breath and then sat his tea down.

"That's why you're here. You're having trouble remembering certain things. We've been using different techniques to try to help you remember. I would have liked to have started therapy long before, but your neurologist was adamant about allowing your brain to heal first."

"I'd like to try something different this week since the tea didn't seem to jog any sense memories. I'd like to hypnotize you. Maybe you can talk more freely then."

I had always thought that hypnotism was a magician's trick, but he seemed to think it would help me. What did I have to lose? If I had known, I would never have nodded my head.

Once I was under, I immediately returned to my apartment where I was sitting on my sofa in the sunlight. I had left Dreamville and I had left Gordon there as well.

Chapter Twenty

When I saw that I was back, I began to weep and run through the apartment. Everything was exactly as it had been before I had fallen in the bathroom. Everything was exactly the same except for the woman. She was gone.

I had spent weeks in Dreamville only to return to the same time that I had gone there. I picked up the towel I had put out and threw it across the small bathroom. I sat down on the cold tile floor next to the claw foot tub and could not stop crying. I had lost him. I had left him in that waiting room and I had known that I wouldn't be coming back through that door to him. I had known it and I still went. I wanted to howl in pain, but all I could produce were soundless sobs that robbed me of my breath.

The pain in my chest from the tears was so hard that I did not think that I would ever feel right again. Could I get back to Dreamville? Could I get back to him? And if I couldn't, how could I hide my feelings from the Gordon I knew here, the man whom I had just thrown out of my apartment? Oh shit, what had I done?

I could call him, I thought, and I ran to grab my cell phone. As I dialed his number, I prayed that he would answer and not decline the call. I was so tired of fighting this battle between Dreamville and the real world. At that moment, I just wanted him, no matter what reality was true.

He answered on the third ring with a terse "Yes".

"Gordon, Mr. Stewart, I want to apologize for my behavior this morning. I can't explain it and I'll understand if you're angry with me, but . . . I truly cannot tell you just how sorry I am."

Silence on the other end. Gordon in Dreamville was silent like that, especially when he was angry with me. What could I say? I tried to think of anything that would turn the situation around. And that triggered a memory in my head that I had not remembered – the word situation flashed an image of a fist coming at my face and the feel of pain filling my cheekbone.

"Cheekbone," I said. I became so lost in the image that I did not hear his voice on the phone.

I looked around the apartment and felt myself falling to the floor, watching the cell phone slip from my hand. It was as if the entire moment was in slow motion and my last thought as I lost consciousness was what had the image meant?

I came to in Dreamville. Dr. Fritcher was shaking me and Gordon was next to me, trying to calm me down. I didn't realize that the screaming I was hearing was coming from me until I closed my mouth.

I could feel my face was wet with tears and when I realized that Gordon was in front of me, I threw my arms around him and begged him to take me home. He looked up at Dr. Fritcher, who shook his head.

"I'm going back to the waiting room, April. You'll be fine now. I promise to be waiting there for you," Gordon said.

I became frantic. No, if he left, I might leave again, too. I didn't want to go back to the real world. I wanted to stay in Dreamville.

He pulled his arms from me and quickly left the room.

Dr. Fritcher handed me a glass of water and a small blue pill.

"What is this?"

"It's a Valium. It will help you relax a little bit before we finish up for the day. You had quite a breakthrough. Do you remember?"

I pondered the tiny blue pill and thought of the scene in the movie *The Matrix* where the hero is offered the blue pill or the red pill. I tossed the blue pill in my mouth and took a deep swallow of the water.

What did I remember? I remembered being hypnotized. I woke to find myself in the real world and immediately wondered if I should start referring to it as the other world. I was talking to the older Gordon when I had flashed on the image of the fist crashing into my face. But I said very little of this to Dr. Fritcher.

"I remember a fist hitting my cheekbone. That's it."

I was quiet for a moment and then looked up at the doctor.

"If I were in an accident, why did I remember that?"

He leaned back in his armchair and tapped his pencil on his tablet.

"That's a good question, April. Maybe you need to think about why you're here and what might have happened to bring you here?"

I felt cold suddenly and could not erase the image of that fist coming at my face. I closed my eyes and tried to see the fist clearly. It was tan and there was a large gold ring on it with a dark brown stone.

I told this to Dr. Fritcher and he hurriedly wrote down what I was telling him on his notepad.

"This will help, April. I'll call . . ." then he stopped himself midsentence.

"I'll call you to check up on you this week and I'll see you next week at the same time," he said as he took my hands and raised me to my feet and led me to the waiting room door.

"I'd like to speak to Gordon for a moment, so if you'd just have a seat here for a few seconds," he said as he waved Gordon into his office.

"Wait," I said. "Shouldn't my family be involved in this?"

His expression did not change except for a small squint of his eyes.

"Why, April, you know that they've trusted everything to Gordon and you. They know how strong your relationship is with him."

I nodded and sat down, but I still did not really understand. I also had no idea what he discussed with Gordon, but Gordon came out smiling tightly.

"Shall we go down to Little Italy to Benito's and have a nice lunch, dear? I'm thinking of their squid ink pasta with scallops. What about you?"

I returned his smile, but said nothing. I wasn't very hungry, but I suddenly saw another overlap from the other world – Benito's. It was where I first met him in that world, but in this world it seemed as if it were somewhere we often ate.

As we drove downtown toward Mulberry Street and the few blocks of Little Italy that had not become part of Chinatown near Mott Street, I closed my eyes and tried to remember more about what had happened at the doctor's office. Would my family really leave me to Gordon's care if something traumatic had happened to me? Knowing my father, I could not believe it was true. I tried to remember the last time I had spoken with him. Surely it hadn't been that long ago. Why had I only spoken with my brother, Lisa, or Gordon in either Dreamville or the real world?

For some reason, my mind turned to Gordon's apartment and the fact that Frank said we had moved there only a month ago. Had something happened a little over a month ago?

"Gordon, who decorated the apartment?"

"The flat? Why you did most of it, but we made quite a few decisions together. Why do you ask?"

"Gordon, Frank said we'd only been there a month. How could we make a home that looked like that in a month?"

His face flushed and he turned away from me briefly, then grinned at me.

"Why Frank probably meant when we actually moved there, not when we bought it and began work on it."

He grinned, but his eyes were not smiling. He was lying to me or else he was not telling me everything. And I knew deep in my bones that what he was hiding had something to do with both the fist crashing into my face and my lack of communication with my parents.

I just had to remember. I had to work hard at it. My sanity seemed to balance on it. Either Dreamville was real or the other world was. And that was when a chilling thought came to me – my family, other than Rick and Lisa, were not on vacation.

And, of course, that was when I blacked out in the back seat of his town car.

I could hear his voice, and once more found myself standing in my kitchen with my cell phone. The world had shifted again.

Just when I would start to think of something in either place, I would wind up in the opposite. Meanwhile, I had Gordon calling my name on the phone. I clicked off the phone call and walked to my bedroom, holding the phone in my hand.

Did I dare do it? Would the results be the same as in Dreamville? I pulled up the contact screen and touched my parents name.

And the same recording I had heard in Dreamville, repeated in my ear – the number was not a working number.

Chapter Twenty-One

And once again, I found myself being shook awake by Gordon.

"April, April, wake up. April?"

I could feel the world coming back into focus and found myself in the backseat of the town car, my body slumped over into Gordon's lap. I felt dizzy, but I tried to sit up and Gordon helped lift me up.

"Maybe we should just get take out," he said. "I don't think going out is a good idea, but you probably do need to eat something. You've been through quite a bit this morning."

I nodded my head and leaned against his shoulder. Would I ever know the truth? I felt an overwhelming sense of loss. I didn't think I could find my family anymore than I had been able to find my business or my apartment building in Soho. I only had Gordon, Rick and Lisa. I was beginning to believe that nothing was real, not Dreamville, not my real world, not even my memories of what may or may not have been.

The only thing that I did know was that I loved Gordon. I had no idea if he were a product of my imagination or if I was seriously ill or, if, for not the first time, I wondered whether or not I might be dead. There seemed to be no way to reconcile the two worlds.

I tried again to approach everything that was happening and had happened logically. I mentally ticked off everything in my head as we headed up Fifth Avenue. I still could not come up with any sensible solution by the time we reached Gordon's.

I wandered off the elevator and to his, our bedroom and laid down upon the comforter, rolling on my side to look out the window at the rain which was falling now instead of snow. The wind blew the water against the windowpanes and the tracks of the rivulets were shadowed against the wall by the low afternoon light.

I had always loved New York in every season, but this winter it was just a landscape of gray stone. I could not see anything other than the surrounding buildings from where I was on the bed and I didn't think that anything would make things worse.

Dr. Fritcher seemed to think that I had made a "breakthrough" that morning, but I didn't feel as if I had. If nothing, I felt worse and more confused than I had before the visit to his office. I wondered if I wanted to be in this world or what I had been calling my real world. I only knew that I needed Gordon in either place.

What puzzled me the most was why I had fixed on myself at the age on the ages I had. At first I had traveled to my 16th year and then my 19th, but now I only moved back and forth from 25 to 32. Why did everything at 25 seem like a dream? Could this be the life I had wanted and not lived? Or could 32 be Dreamville?

No, I thought, my memories of 32 were too clear, too detailed. But, then I thought, so were the aspects of life here. I brushed tears away from my face fearing that I might be stuck at either moment in time, never moving forward, never living again, and always being torn from one place to another.

The light next to the bed came on and I rolled over to find Gordon there with a tray with plates overflowing with sandwiches and two cans of Coke.

"Sit up and scoot," he said.

I smiled at him and wiped my face with the back of my hand. He handed me a plate loaded with a giant sandwich of roast turkey, cheddar cheese, and ham surrounded by potato chips. I took a bite of the sandwich and realized just how hungry I was. I started to eat quickly and reached across his lap to grab one of the Cokes to drink.

He laughed and held his plate up in the air as if I were going to eat his sandwich as well.

"I didn't know we had any soda, but this is so good. I can't remember the last time I had a non-diet soda," I said.

"We didn't, but I thought that your dizziness might be low blood sugar so I ordered regular Cokes to go with our sandwiches."

I nodded and continued to devour the sandwich and chips. And I did start to perk up.

"I feel like we're having a picnic on the bed, especially with this dreary rain."

He had finished his lunch too and placed both plates on the tray. He crawled over to me and held himself above me.

"And you know what the best part of a picnic on the bed is?" he asked, as he took one hand and began to unbutton my blouse.

"Oh, I can think of a few things," I replied.

He kissed my breasts where he had opened my blouse and a small moan escaped my mouth.

"The best part is that we don't have to go anywhere to be alone. We can stay right here as long as we want," he said.

I lifted my head from the pillow and kissed him, tasting the salty sweetness of our lunch on his lips. He pulled my body to his and we spent the rest of the afternoon in the bed, our bodies entangled, driving away the cold rain outside.

"I love you, April Norris. I have since we were 16. I think I always will. You're not the easiest person to know, but you are the love of my life," he said.

I had never had any man say anything like that to me. I thought it was something that people only said in books or movies. I wrapped my arms around his neck and held on for the ride of my life. I decided that no matter what happened, that I was going to love this man forever. How could I not?

Chapter Twenty-Two

It seemed as if Dreamville had become my only world as the weeks went by. February turned into March and the weather was typically New York in late winter - windy, rainy and miserable. But unlike the month of March, I was not miserable. I had accepted my fate of spending the rest of my life in Dreamville. Not that I would ever tell anyone. Not Gordon or Rick and Lisa or my doctors. Gordon never mentioned the wedding again. But for reasons upon which I did not want to dwell, it didn't bother me much. It didn't feel right to talk about it. Talking about it frightened me in an odd way.

I also stopped thinking about the real world. After a few attempts at trying to get anyone to talk to me about my family without success, I also stopped asking about them. Something in the back of my brain told me to shut up. It was as if the question became the scary thing on the steps of the third floor of my parents' home, something that would end me. So I chose blissful ignorance, also knowing that it would not last either. I could feel something creeping toward me, especially the nights after my sessions with Dr. Fritcher. I would awaken and reach out for Gordon's form in the big bed and would crawl over to him and hug his back, holding on to him as if he would be taken away from me at any moment.

We spent most of our time alone together in the apartment. He would go into his library and work most days. He said he didn't want to leave me alone in the apartment and that he could work from home for a little longer. I should have asked questions then, but I didn't. I was so blindly in love with him that fear kept me conveniently quiet.

Only one time did I broach the subject of his work and he dismissed it with his usual shrug and smile.

"You mean you just want me conveniently near," I responded to his enigmatic answer by teasing him to come to me.

He would laugh and take the hint and we would spend our afternoons making love. Once I accepted my fate in Dreamville, I embraced it with a fervor that surprised me. We made love in almost every room of the house, everywhere except for his library, which seemed to be off limits. I once thought of the room that the heroine of the fairy tale was forbidden to enter or she would suffer a terrible fate. It's not that I had never seen inside the room, but I had never entered it. It, too, gave me the feeling I had felt as a child about the third floor of my parents' home.

Once I asked Gordon what he did in there and he said, "Argue with lawyers," which I thought was odd since Rick took care of those things, but I never asked. It was as if I were living in a fragile glass shell that would burst if I pushed against the walls of it.

I longed for him as I had never wanted anyone or anything in my life. Thus, Dreamville became my real world and the real world was slowly disappearing with the month of March.

Sometimes Rick and Lisa joined us for supper. One night Rick announced Lisa's first pregnancy and I hoped for her sake that Dreamville would not follow the rules of the world I rarely visited anymore. In that world, she had lost two babies before Baby David was born healthy and exactly on time.

The night they informed us of the pregnancy I wept in Gordon's arms without knowing why. Once again, that wall formed around my questions and emotions as if to protect me. By this time, I was becoming more and more accepting of Dr. Fritcher's explanation of a memory loss that would return and that I should not try to force it by asking those around me questions that might make my world a dark and unforgiving place.

Strangely enough, when I cried that night, Gordon never questioned the tears. He kissed my eyelids, wiped the tears away, and held me tightly, almost preventing me from moving. I supposed that maybe he was thinking my tears were for not having a child with him, but I could never tell him the truth – that I thought I was living in a place called Dreamville, a place that could vanish with the rising sun. My greatest fear in those months was that he would leave me. I feared that telling the truth would end everything and by this time I loved him so much that I could not risk that he would desert me.

I never questioned that we rarely left the apartment or that he seemed to always be nearby, that my family might not be traveling abroad, that he had seemingly appeared from nowhere and had become the center around which my life revolved. There were times when I was alone when I allowed a glimmer of these questions to surface like a rock skittering across the face of a lake, but like the skittering rock, I pushed the questions deep into the lake of my subconscious, hoping to eventually forget them, sinking to the bottom of my memory like the items in the darkness of Jackson Pollack's *Full Fathom Five*.

I did remember seeing that painting at MoMA on a field trip my sophomore year of high school. The painting had fascinated me, repelled me, and had drawn me into it. Looking at it made me feel as if I were drowning, but in some way it also made me feel finally safe and hidden away from the world.

I could remember that trip and other events in my life before my first visit to Dreamville and my first sight of Gordon in my high school hall. Those memories I did not doubt. They were very real. Sometimes not as detailed as what I was supposed to be remembering, but real nevertheless.

By the first of April, the daffodils were blooming in the park and I began to clean up the debris on the terrace and plan on furnishing the terrace with plants and items beyond the single stone bench on it. Whenever I went out there, I noticed that Gordon left his work and either stood in the doorway or joined me outside. I once wondered if he were afraid that I might fall from there, but I said nothing as I wanted him with me. My real world was falling away faster and faster and that both comforted and confused me. I knew that I had either lived a life or dreamed a life without him. I just couldn't face the possibility of that world now.

And, of course, that's when life changes and leaves you standing alone in the dark, frightened, speechless, and without hope – when you dare to be happy, unquestioning, and hopeful.

After months of waking up in our bed next to him, I went back to the real world and found myself alone. I awoke in my old apartment in my old iron bed with my grandmother's quilt wrapped around me like a shroud. I had been lost in that real world and he had found me in Dreamville. And now I was lost again.

Instead of breaking into tears, I saw the futility in fighting whatever was happening to me. I decided to go into work that morning and as I was drinking my coffee, my cell phone rang. It had been so long since I had heard it that at first I wasn't sure what I was hearing. By the time I found it in the living room, the *Tiny Dancer* ringtone had stopped and I saw that I had missed a call from Lisa. That was also when I noticed the date and saw that once more I had gone back to January 8th. I sat down on my sofa and thought of Gordon. Where was he today? What was he doing? Who was with him?

I took a deep breath, put the phone in my purse and went to work. The day was cold and snow was whirling around the street like dust devils. I kept telling myself to just hold on, that I would be back with him soon, and that if not, I could love him in this world and maybe, just maybe he could love me as well.

So, it was a great surprise when he quickly entered my shop with Lisa, as another woman walked briskly ahead of Lisa. She chattered away with Lisa about all the beautiful antiques in my shop. I never looked at either of the women.

Gordon was the sole focus of my attention. I smiled at him as if he were the Gordon I loved in Dreamville and not the stranger standing before me.

"I know we should have made an appointment with you, but she wouldn't wait," he said.

I smiled and said it was ok and that I understood Lisa's need to get out now and then. I gazed into his grey eyes and hoped that he would see me there before him and some spark would ignite, something, anything, would bring him to me.

"Oh, I'm sure Lisa is very happy to be out, but I meant Charlotte, my fiancée," he said and my world collapsed.

"She just arrived from Edinburgh yesterday and she's appalled at the condition of my flat."

Somehow I managed to maintain a smile as he continued to praise her, but all I could do was think of his arms wrapped around me, the picnic on our bed, our lovemaking on the marble table in the foyer. All I could do was nod and smile. I was thinking that my life was over when Lisa walked back to my counter where Gordon was speaking of his Charlotte when I saw her face for the first time and I saw the face of the woman from the hospital, the woman from my nightmares, the woman who had dared me to speak lest I be killed.

And that was when I began to scream.

Chapter Twenty-Three

When I screamed, I closed my eyes, thinking that I would awaken in Dreamville, but instead I found myself in my childhood bedroom once more and Gordon's Charlotte was standing over me with a revolver in her hand.

She slapped me hard enough to jar my teeth and hissed, "Bitch, shut up or you'll be dead, too."

I felt my lower jaw ache and moved it back and forth reflexively

I could hear screams in the house. It sounded like my mother. Oh god, I thought. What fresh nightmare had I found myself in? But, I knew that this was the dark thing that had been hiding inside me. I thought that Charlotte was death come to claim me, that my time in Dreamville was just a prelude, a sweet and last coma dream that my poor brain had gifted to me.

I tried to crawl away from her, but my hands and feet were tied together behind my back. From where I was lying in the floor, I could see that my mother had begun storing long boxes of Christmas decorations beneath my bed. I remembered that she always stored the ornaments there. They were easy to get to each year and easy to take downstairs to use to decorate the house for the holidays. For some reason, I focused on a small glass ornament shaped as an orange and I recalled that I had just brought that box of decorations up from the downstairs and had pushed the box under the bed when I had heard the doorbell ring.

And that was when I realized that this was the real world and my memory returned. Dreamville and what I had called my "real" world were just attempts at escaping the truth of what had happened when our door bell rang.

I remembered I had gone to the staircase and I saw two men and a woman push my grandmother down onto the floor. The three of them were carrying guns and one of the men casually pointed his gun at my grandmother's chest and pulled the trigger. I crouched down below the stair rail and watched as a beautiful, bright red rose bloomed against her chest. Her body went limp as the rose grew and overflowed onto the cream marble floor of the foyer. She had fallen next to an ebony settee and I remembered marveling at how the rose matched the thin red stripe in the upholstered seat of the settee.

My family came running into the wide hallway, my brothers appearing first, with David leading the way, Carl close behind him. I heard the gun fire again, the sound echoing up the stairwell to where I hid.

The man who had shot my grandmother had aimed the gun at David as he ran into the hall. He had casually raised the gun and pulled the trigger. I watched as David crumpled to the ground like a marionette whose strings had been cut.

The man was aiming the gun at Carl when I began to scream and this time I needed no prompting to know the scream was coming from my mouth.

The man hit Carl's head with the butt of the gun and Carl fell next to my mother's feet, his body twitching as if he were having a seizure. My mother was screaming with me in some weird cacophonous harmony. The man struck her across the face with his open hand, which silenced her and caused me to close my mouth as well. He said something to the woman and she bounded up the stairs towards me.

She used her gun to propel me down to where the rest of my family was. My father had placed his hand over my mother's mouth and had pulled her close against his chest to keep her eyes averted from her hurt children.

"Where's the safe?" the man who had been doing the shooting asked.

He looked so normal, like a person you'd see in a shopping mall somewhere instead of a man with a gun who had just killed my grandmother and brother. I thought at that moment that perhaps I was in shock. I could not accept what was happening in my home. None of it was real.

As he grabbed my father, I could see my father's arms shaking and hear my father's voice tremble as he spoke.

"I don't have one, but you can take what you want. Here, just don't hurt anyone else. Take our jewelry," he said as he removed his Rolex and his wedding ring.

"Take anything you want. We'll cooperate with you. I swear. Just leave my family alone."

The other man grabbed the jewelry and threw it into a Christmas shopping bag he was carrying. The shopping bag was striped green and gold and had a shiny cartoon on it of a Santa holding his belly. The Santa was laughing with a cartoon cloud that read "Ho, Ho Ho". The man with the bag looked around the room and grinned.

"Looks like we're going to get some great Christmas presents tonight since Santa skipped us."

I was trying to edge my way along the wall to where Carl was lying in the floor when the woman yanked my long hair and threw me backwards onto the floor and I slid on the marble that I saw was slippery from the blood flowing from David's head.

David, 22 years old. Dead, his blood forming a second rose under his head.

The woman rifled through David's pockets first and removed his wallet and then the school ring from his hand. She tossed them into the shopping bag and then headed over to Carl.

Just as she pulled his wallet from his pocket, he began to moan. The first man nodded at Carl and then to the man with the bag. The Santa man grinned again and placed the nozzle of the gun against Carl's temple and pulled the trigger. Carl's smile was gone forever.

I had curled up in a far corner and begun to cry. One by one, I was watching these people kill my family. It was January 8th, shortly after New Year's Day, and we had been taking down the Christmas decorations. I realized as I lie curled there that I would never see a Christmas again and I cried even harder.

The first man told the woman and the man with the bag to take me upstairs and tie me up. Before they did, he walked over to me and knelt before me. He touched my chin, lifted my face and smiled. And God, oh God, I wanted to go back to Dreamville so much at that moment.

I looked at his face and I recognized those heather blue-grey eyes from so many nights together in Dreamville. He leaned closer and whispered in my ear with a softly accented voice, "Now, go be a good girl and I might take you with me."

I looked at the woman and saw the Charlotte woman turn into Lisa and saw that the Santa man with the shopping bag turn into the man whom I had been calling Rick, the man I had thought was my brother. I knew then that I had no other brothers except for Carl and David and now they were dead.

It was as if everything suddenly clicked into place.

How could I have deluded myself? Was this how my poor brain had protected me, by giving me a dream of months of love in the last seconds of tragedy?

The people in Dreamville and my "real" world, the people in Dreamville who had refused to tell me anything about my parents, were actually the people who had invaded my home and murdered my family.

I stumbled to my feet and took one last, long look at my doomed parents. I knew that it would be my mother's scream I would hear in my bedroom as she watched them kill my father, and then the eerie silence that followed a second gun shot.

And that was where I was when the woman I had been seeing as a faceless nightmare for what had felt like months had cursed me. I was staring at a glass orange fruit ornament in a long plastic box underneath my bed.

It didn't take long for the men to ransack the downstairs before I heard their footsteps on the staircase heading towards my bedroom.

The man I had called Gordon, the man I had thought I had loved, the man who had murdered my grandmother and David, waved the Lisa/Charlotte creature and the Rick/Santa man from the room, ordering them to search the rest of the house.

The woman looked none too happy, but she did as he said. The man I had called Gordon bent down and grabbed the ropes and dragged me toward the third floor door.

The ascent was not an easy one and each step made me realize why I had feared that place. As we rounded the landing to the few steps before the hall leading to the bedrooms, I could hear the other two downstairs as they went through the rooms looking for valuables.

The Gordon man dragged my body to the first bedroom. Somehow he had managed to break my left elbow and cut my face as he had let my body bounce against each step and turn in the staircase.

He took out a knife and cut the rope from my feet, but left my hands bound. He lifted me into the air by jerking the ropes that firmly kept my arms tied behind my back. He threw me onto my bed and laid me there face up, forcing me to watch as he sliced at the waistband of my pants. His movements were slow and languorous, like those of a man about to make love, some of the same movements that I had seen Gordon make so many times in Dreamville before he made love to me.

The knife sliced easily through the fabric and I felt him spread my legs as he cut my panties off and then the front of my sweater. He took the tip of the knife and slid it across where my breasts were.

"You are so beautiful. I don't know if I've ever touched someone so delicate. Are you pure? Let me look at you," he said and touched me with his fingers, gently caressing me before inserting his fingers into my vagina.

"Oh, you are pure! I promise it won't hurt but for a second and then you'll love it."

He lowered his mouth to my breasts and kissed my chest, my belly, and finally placing one last kiss on the inside of my thigh.

I never looked away from his eyes, even as he removed his clothes. I had seen his body so many times in Dreamville that the beauty of it was no surprise to me.

He climbed onto the bed and guided himself into me. As he was raised over me, we locked our eyes with one another. I would not look away. For some reason, that made him smile. He did not know that the reason I would not look away was that I wanted to see Gordon in there somewhere, if only one last time.

As he raped me, all I could think of was the man I had loved in Dreamville. I did not cry as he assaulted me. I felt a tearing and a wetness in my crotch as he slowly moved back and forth inside me, each stroke, for me, mixing pain with pleasure, terror with the terrible acceptance of the truth of the situation.

I tried not to weep as he thrust into me. I tried to think of the life I had never lived, the life Dreamville had given me. I had not realized that I had fallen in love with Death.

As he had thrown me onto the bed, I had seen my reflection in the mirror of the dresser and had seen that I was 25 years old. I was a virgin that January night.

Instead of the lives I had had in Dreamville and the fake "real" world, I had stayed at home with my parents. There had been no Columbia, no Vince, no men. I had joined my mother in her quilt shop and had enjoyed the quiet company of women and books. Everything that I had thought was real, everything I had thought was Dreamville was false, a hope of a life that I might have had.

I watched his eyes close tightly and knew the end was coming. His last act as he climaxed was to bring his fist down into my face, completing the final puzzle piece by breaking my cheek bone. I knew then why I had said "cheekbone" under hypnosis in Dreamville.

As he finished with me, I lie there and watched as he picked up the gun from the night stand. I felt the barrel of his gun at against my chest. He, my Gordon, my love, my myth, shrugged and smiled as he kissed me tenderly. I wanted him to love me as I could not help but love him. My delusion, my heart's desire.

Death, my lover, kissed me one last time and I was gone.

ABOUT THE AUTHOR

Reneé Porter is the author of the series of novels, **The Taliaferro Chronicles**, including *The 13th Victim* and *Redemption Ridge*, as well as the novel, *Bell Park*. *Dreamville* is her fourth novel.

Reneé Porter